"The New Zealander. Everyone talks about you. All the women, anyway," Desi said.

"Yeah?" Tam grinned. Slowly.

Desi looked weary. "Do me a favor. Save the charm for somebody else. I'm not charmable."

He raised an eyebrow. A challenge he couldn't possibly resist. "That sounds like throwing down a gauntlet to me."

For one instant, Desi suddenly felt aware of her lips, of her breasts, her throat. Her hands, so capable, felt awkward at the ends of her arms, and as she stood there a wave of dizzy awareness moved down her spine. He was absolutely stunning.

A great reason to give him wide berth. Gorgeous men were more trouble than they were worth, as her now-late husband Claude had so brilliantly illustrated.

"Trust me," she said, rocking back on her heels. "It's not."

Dear Reader,

A couple of years ago, I had a sudden and unexpected opportunity to visit New Zealand, and it turned out to be a dazzling experience, unlike anywhere I'd ever been—or even will be again. Everything about the place enchanted me, drifts of calla lilies growing wild in the field, the look of icy-green ferns unfurling, a kind of wood that can lie underground for centuries and still not rot! I wandered around in a state of love-struck wonder, and I guarantee you I will be going back.

This book is not about New Zealand exactly—I'll leave that to the New Zealanders themselves—but it was born when I was sitting with my friends one afternoon in a Rotorua street, eating ice cream cones with the smell of sulfur in the air. A man walked by, sturdy and healthy and fulsomely beautiful in his skin, and I could not help but admire him. Okay—I admit it—I stared. You would have, too. He enjoyed being admired, gave me a little wink, and walked on. I have not forgotten New Zealand and all its magic, nor that dashing man so delighted by the day and his beauty, a day a seed of a book was planted.

Ruth Wind

RUTH WIND

Desi's Rescue

Silhouette®
Romantic
SUSPENSE

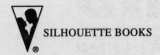

SILHOUETTE BOOKS
®

ISBN-13: 978-0-373-27529-8
ISBN-10: 0-373-27529-3

DESI'S RESCUE

Books by Ruth Wind

RUTH WIND

A passionate hiker and traveler, Ruth Wind likes nothing better than setting off at dawn for a trip—anywhere! Her favorite places so far include the Tasman Sea off the coast of New Zealand, the aromatic and pungent streets of New York City and the top of her beloved Pikes Peak. Between books, she's currently planning trips to India, China and a long rest in the damp and misty United Kingdom. Explore her columns on rambling around France and Scotland, working the marathon to the top of Pikes Peak and many topics about the writing life at awriterafoot.com.

Ruth Wind also writes women's fiction under the name Barbara Samuel. You can visit her Web site at www.barbarasamuel.com.

This one is dedicated with fondness to Frances Housden, who dazzled me with New Zealand.

Prologue

November

No one noticed the woman as she walked in the dark shadows of the street that lay behind the Thunderbird Casino. The giant gambling facility stood right beyond the imaginary line that divided the town of Mariposa from the Mariposa Ute Indian reservation, but it seemed to be part of the town of Mariposa itself, situated as it was at the end of Black Diamond Boulevard.

The town had insisted there be no light pollution marring the romance of a high-mountain night in the village, and as a result, the casino's noise and lights were contained within a large warehouse-sized building cleverly and artistically designed to look like a series of storefronts. It even had a long porch with a roof, a popular place for tourists to perch on summer evenings.

Cold had driven everyone inside tonight, and the woman waited in the spiky shadows beneath a stand of aspens and pines for her quarry to emerge, a revolver heavy and cold in her pocket. She'd seen him go in. Eventually he would come out. She was patient.

When Claude Tsosie emerged, he had a woman at his side. Not at all unusual, since he nearly always had a woman at his side, one about to be charmed or one who had fallen or one hoping he would give her one more day, one more hour.

Tonight the woman was Christie Lundgren, a skier who'd taken the silver medal at Turin. The athletic and spoiled Christie had fallen for the charming Native American artist like a pitch down an icy slope. A shame. The woman waiting in the cold shadows hated to see the girl waste herself on such a loser. Claude would toy with her, string her along and break her heart. He might even ruin Christie's chances to take the gold next time.

A waste.

Just as Claude was a waste. He betrayed everyone, sooner or later.

Not for much longer.

The woman bided her time, watching patiently as Claude tucked Christie into her car—obviously against her protests—with a kiss, then headed off toward his own truck, parked a little farther on. He whistled under his breath.

The woman moved. Out of the darkness, into the light. "Hello, Claude," she said calmly. She could be charming when she wished and she knew what he liked.

Startled, he looked up at her, covering his initial dismay with a quick, practiced smile. "Hey," he said, reaching for her arm. "How are you?"

"Will you walk with me, just for a minute? I need to talk to you."

He didn't want to. She could see that. "I'm supposed to be somewhere. How about tomorrow morning?"

She inclined her head, letting her hair fall in an alluring line down her arm. "It won't take long." She glanced over her shoulder, as if worried they would be seen together. "I think it will be profitable for both of us."

And as always, his arrogance overruled his instincts. He slammed shut the door to his truck, buttoned his coat and took her arm. "Sure, baby. Let's take a little walk."

Chapter 1

February

He found the wolf cub howling as if the world had ended. Which, for the cub, he supposed it had.

Tam Neville tried not to brood. It was a waste and a shame, his grandfather had told him, to spend the precious hours of a life complaining or grousing or doing anything less than celebrating the world the gods had made. In theory, Tam agreed.

But sometimes even he had a bad night. So when morning came he took himself into the mountains. His passion was for running, an ardor he could not overcome even with a bum leg and a dozen reasons he should give it up. He could not imagine a life without running in it.

Unfortunately, during the cold, snowy winters in Mariposa, running was impossible, so he slapped on snowshoes and headed into the high-mountain forests and meadows. It kept him in shape, kept his demolished knee from solidifying entirely, kept his lungs at full power.

On this pale pink and gray morning, the air was so sharp and cold and still that his breath hung in commas. Until he'd stumbled into the clearing, Tam had been focused on the feeling of crisp mountain air opening his lungs, sending power through his limbs. Even now, when his speed had been cut in half and he sometimes hobbled more than ran—sometimes paying the price later with aching knees and back—he loved the invigoration of hard exercise. It was a through-line in his life—running around the shores of the turquoise Tasman Sea, through the forests near his grandfather's home and across parks and rugby fields.

Snowshoeing worked his legs, his chest, his arms, and the unbroken stillness of thickly blanketed mountains eased the restless heat in his soul. The snow was so deep that it was a glacial blue in the holes alongside tree trunks. He could imagine he was one of the explorer heroes of his childhood, like Magellan or Cook or Vespucci, breaking through frontiers never before explored.

He'd had a bad night, triggered by a long hand-holding session with the young widow of his late best friend Roger, a fellow smoke jumper who had died in the same incident that had mangled Tam's left leg. Zara's sobs had kept him up late, and then this morning Tam had heard the news that Elsa, his ex-girlfriend, had married the businessman she'd been angling to catch. A smaller loss, that, but still a bit of a pain.

Stinging with losses large and small, Tam came out into the opalescent brilliance of a February mountain morning to run his sorrows to ground.

It didn't take long for his natural optimism to re-assert itself. As the owner of the Black Crown, a pub in the ski town of Mariposa, he had a reputation as a genial man with a big, hearty laugh. Men liked his Kiwi accent and the vigorous, international air he lent the main street of the ski town. Women liked his thick dark curls, which he kept just long enough to amuse them, his green eyes, his easy smile.

Elsa, Elsa, Elsa. He shook his head. He didn't necessarily know what he'd seen in her except her extraordinary beauty. Which could, after all, only take you so far. He supposed it was his pride that had been bruised as much as anything.

The snowshoes swished across the top of the snow. His thighs pumped to carry him up the mountain. Sweat poured down his spine.

Last spring Elsa had wandered into the Black Crown, nearly six feet of long-haired, blond astonishment. Quite to his surprise, Tam had fallen. Hard. He told himself it was because she represented all those out-of-reach girls from his youth who'd disdained what now was sexy—his dark half-Maori exoticness.

He'd told himself it would never last, that she was on the prowl for a rich man, a very, *very* rich man, and that she had the cunning and beauty required to snare one.

He'd told himself she'd make his life a merry chase and he didn't need the headache.

He'd told himself many things. And not really believed any of them.

Now she had married her rich man. Her very, *very* rich developer husband, twice her age. Tam paused to take a long swallow of cold water from the pack on his back. Was it his heart that was wounded, he wondered, or his pride? He didn't know anymore. Elsa was so different from the usual sort of woman he picked that it seemed something had to be at work.

After a few miles the heat in his lungs began to ease away, and he circled a favorite meadow, a wide-open bowl of pristine snow above a sacred shrine called Our Lady of the Butterflies. Some anomaly of temperature—perhaps the hot springs that ran through the area—made the glade and waterfall a haven for butterflies, and even in the coldest months of January and February, one sometimes saw mourning cloak butterflies flitting about. He kept his eyes open. It was a wonder, that was sure—seeing one of the delicate black butterflies landing on the snow.

Crossing the meadow above the falls, he heard the howl.

Unmistakably the howl of a wolf. He halted and looked around carefully but saw nothing. The bawling cry sounded again—a little ragged—was it a pup? Tam scowled. If there *was* a cub in danger, there might be adults who wouldn't care for his presence. He didn't fancy a torn throat.

The cry came again, heartrending. Tam ventured into the clearing gingerly, looking around. Nothing. Only a wide expanse of unbroken snow, possibly six or seven feet deep—maybe more. They were saying it was one of the best ski seasons in thirty years.

No cub.

He moved around the perimeter, listening, his instincts pricked. His training as a smoke jumper had taught him how to manage injured animals. He'd learned to be wary of them and watchful. This hidden one had that sound—a small animal in pain. He waded farther into the powdery snow.

The howl bawled out again into the morning air, and Tam caught sight of something in a hollow between rocks. There was something about it that made him think it might be the hidden entrance to a den, and he approached cautiously. Obviously, there were no parents about, or they'd have nudged the babe along somewhere else.

A movement caught Tam's eye, and he whirled to see a very young cub, black-faced with a gray body, hobble out into the open, as if appealing for help. A bloody mark marred its left haunch. Tam cursed. It had been shot, but not badly, he didn't think. By the grace of God, it was only grazed, but sore enough for that.

"Ah, you poor thing," he said, and took off his shirt then put his coat back on.

Creeping close, he captured the pup in his shirt,

wrapped him tight and kept the baby's mouth far away. It showed no inclination to bite him, however, but let go of an exhausted sigh that nearly ripped Tam's heart right out of his chest.

Rigging up a sling inside his coat, Tam cradled the babe close to his body and headed down the mountain. There was a wildlife refuge just outside of town. He'd take the pup there.

It wasn't until he was down the mountain, putting the baby in the seat of his four-wheel drive that he realized the fires in his chest had been quenched to nothing.

Desdemona Rousseau had been a vet long enough to know that you couldn't save every animal. Death was natural, and although it brought with it a sting, a world without it would quickly become unlivable. She respected the cycle of life.

But she hated murder, and the female wolf who had just died despite Desi's best efforts had definitely been murdered, cut down by gunshot. An ice fisherman had brought the creature in, unconscious and bleeding, and Desi had known that to save her was likely impossible, but she'd tried anyway.

With acute weariness, Desi stripped off her latex gloves and dropped them in the trash. Later a crew would come in and help her get the body ready to be shipped to a facility for students, and a volunteer would be in to help feed the wolves, but for now she was alone, and glad of it.

The call had come in before dawn. Not that

she'd been sleeping. That was a rare and unusual commodity over the past three months, since her almost-ex-husband, Claude, had been murdered on a cold November night. Desi had originally been arrested for the crime, largely because there had not been enough evidence to arrest anyone else. In the end, the circumstantial case hadn't been enough to keep her in jail and she'd been released, but she was still the main suspect. The police watched her. The town, once so warm and supportive, was suspicious of her. If it wasn't for the wolves and this sanctuary, Desi would want a fresh start somewhere else.

Not that she could leave, either. Not until she was cleared completely of Claude's murder.

Maybe it was the lack of sleep making her feel so despairing and upset over the wolf, she thought, wandering through the empty clinic to the wooden porch that wrapped around the entire building. It was lined with motel-style metal rockers in many colors Desi picked up, here and there, from garage sales. Now that people knew she liked them, they brought them to her. This morning, feeling winded, she ignored the chairs and sank down on the steps.

A vet did not cry over every animal, but this time Desi put her head down on her arms and let herself weep for the senselessness of the death. If pressed, she could not have said whether she was crying purely over the wolf or maybe more over the sorry state of her life. But either way, it was a good relief.

Life seemed very hard lately.

As if to reiterate that fact, a drab olive-colored SUV pulled up in front of the clinic. The deputy sheriff who'd been the bane of her life over the past six months hiked up the back of his heavy belt and nodded at Desi. "Mornin'," Gene Nordquist said, tipping his hat. "Have some trouble overnight, did you?"

Desi just looked at him. "What do you want?"

"Just checking up on you, Miz Rousseau. Making sure everything is okay." He pushed the hat back on his forehead, surveyed the land around them, like a bad actor in a bad television drama.

"It's fine." Desi clamped down on her fury, rubbed her face. "Lost a patient, that's all."

He nodded, eyes behind mirrored sunglasses scanning the area as if she were hiding bodies or big stashes of drugs. Desi knew he had three kids under five, a wife who refused to work outside the home and too many bills. This was his only outlet or sense of power, but that didn't mean she had to like him.

"Heard you've had some offers on the land," he said, "and I wouldn't want you to be gettin' any ideas or nothin'."

"Ideas?"

"Selling. Gettin' out of Dodge."

The pressure from two developers—one who wanted the land for a housing development, the other who wanted to increase his land holdings for a resort and spa—had been accelerating over the past few months, but Desi wasn't about to budge. "I'm not selling," she said. Her voice sounded as worn and ragged as she felt. "I'm not going anywhere. I did not kill my ex-husband and the only way to prove that is to stand my ground."

"Oh, I believe you." He flashed a lipless smile.

"Is there anything in particular you want?" Desi asked. "Or can I get on with my day?"

"I reckon I'm done." He glanced over his shoulder as the sound of tires on the gravel came to them. A four-wheel drive Subaru, the omnipresent car of the high country, pulled into the drive. "Looks like you have a job to do. Have a real good day now, Desdemona."

He climbed into his truck, waving at the approaching car. Desi wanted to throw up, but she stood where she was, glaring after the deputy. They wouldn't charge her, but she was still a "person of interest" in the case and she couldn't go anywhere.

Sooner or later something had to give.

Didn't it?

A man climbed out of the Subaru, a bundle clasped to his chest, and against her will, Desi felt a jolt of awakening. He was, in a word, hot. Six foot three if he was an inch, with muscular shoulders and skin the color of lightly toasted bread—which she was able to see because beneath his down jacket he had his shirt off, wrapped around some animal she couldn't see well. Between the bare chest and the high-tech ski pants that showed his powerfully corded legs, she could see he was a serious athlete. Not unusual around here.

Not her usual type. She liked lean, loose-limbed men. But her body didn't seem to care—every cell stood up and saluted as he came toward her.

"Hello!" he said. "I brought you someone."

Oh. The New Zealander, an ex-rugby player. She'd never met him since she didn't drink and so never went to his pub. But everyone talked about the man, and she saw now exactly why. Great cheekbones, thick dark curls, a clean, beautiful way of moving. For one long second, Desi simply stared.

The bundle in his hands wriggled, and she heard a squeaky, soft whine. "Someone?" she echoed.

"I found him, maybe a wolf, eh?" Gently, he peeled back the cloth of what looked to be a T-shirt to show the round head of a baby wolf, so young its ears were still floppy and soft.

It cried out again, a ragged howl, and Desi stepped forward. "Damn," she said, blinking hard to hold back the surprising, sharp tears. "I think I just lost his mom."

The cub lifted his head and let go of a howl, long and piercing, and from the kennels where the pack had been sleeping, came an answering call and another.

Looking over his shoulder the man said, "There's an eerie sound, isn't it?"

"If you're not used to it, it sure can be." Desi moved forward. "Is the baby wounded?"

"A bit. Looks like he might have been grazed but not shot." The big hands, square and strong, easily cradled the small, furry body. The cub whined, but nestled close to the man's belly.

Desi looked at the wolf cub without touching him. "Bring him into the office—" Then she remembered that the mother was inside, and the cub would smell her. "No, we'll have to take him to the house for now, then we'll find him a kennel and get him something to eat."

"Lead the way." She liked the way he held the pup, close to his broad chest, and the reserve in his beautifully cut mouth. His thumb moved over the cub's ear, soothing, smoothing and he met Desi's gaze. "Breaks your heart, eh?"

The man had incredible eyes, penetrating and direct, pale green with gold lights, almost like wolf eyes. For one instant Desi suddenly felt aware of her lips, of her breasts, her throat. Her hands, so capable, felt awkward at the ends of her arms, and as she stood there, exhausted and depressed, a wave of dizzy awareness moved down her spine. Something about the way he held the cub so easily, with the stance of a strong man who looked like some version of a forest god, or maybe the resonant depth of his voice made her feel new, relieved, intrigued.

He was absolutely stunning.

A great reason to give him wide berth. Gorgeous men were more trouble than they were worth, as her now-late husband, Claude, had so brilliantly illustrated.

She turned away. "Yes. Bring the cub." She led the way to a small cottage, while all around them, wolves set up a howl, sending messages to each other, crying out welcome and warning.

Behind her, the New Zealander spoke in soft tones to the cub, his accent rising and falling in a rhythm very unlike American English.

"Where did you find him?" she asked, pushing open the door to the small house. It was a place for a night person to stay, and was suitably simple—just two rooms, a kitchen/living room and a bedroom with a twin bed shoved beneath a window. A potbellied stove provided heat.

"In a meadow up top of the Shrine." He came into the room, stood there looking around. "Where do you want me to put him?"

Desi looked around. She felt enormously tired, weepy, overwhelmed. Not at all her usual attitude. With a powerful effort, she focused on the task at hand and opened a cupboard. From a neat, freshly folded stack, she took out a sheet and spread it out over the coffee table. "Here. Let's take a look at him."

The cub shivered as the New Zealander's T-shirt fell away, and he looked at them miserably, his irises still slightly bluish with his babyhood. "Damn," she said again. "I'm so sorry, sweetie." Gently she touched his body, head to haunches, feeling for marks, wounds, injuries. Aside from the bloody cut on his haunch, already closing, there appeared to be nothing wrong.

"Is he all right?" the man asked.

"I think so. I'm going to run back to the clinic and get a few things—some gauzes and some formula to feed him."

"There's wolf formula?" He grinned. "Like baby milk?"

Desi smiled. "Exactly. I'll go get some for him. Do you mind holding him awhile longer?"

The man picked up the baby and cuddled him close, like a human child. "Could I feed him?"

Desi nodded. Somebody had to. He'd earned it. "But don't get too attached," she added. "He's a wolf, not a dog."

"Got it."

Desi fled. Walking quickly, she told herself it was just her emotional state this morning that made him look so unbelievably appealing, but she knew it wasn't. She liked his size, his eyes, his muscles, his resonant voice, the accent.

But it was his hands, moving so gently, so surely, so protectively over the body of the baby wolf that electrified her.

Don't even think about it, scolded a voice in her head.

She had enough problems: developers after her land; a fluff head who wanted to build a spa next door, thus compromising the wolf sanctuary; a sister getting married and…oh, yes, that pesky little matter of being investigated for the murder of her late husband.

Don't even think about it.

Tam gratefully sat down after the vet left him in the cabin with the pup. In the distance a wolf howled, long and eerie, and the sound raised gooseflesh on his arms, the hackles on his neck—an ancient genetic response. Although, theoretically it wasn't *his* genetics. There were no wolves in New Zealand. No wolves or lions or even rabbits. No native mammals at all, unless you counted sea mammals—seals and so forth.

The pup trembled faintly next to his belly, a soft low whine coming from his throat. The sound just about ripped his heart half out of his chest. "It'll be all right, mate," he murmured, rubbing a velvety ear between his thumb and forefinger. "Sorry about your mum, but we'll get you fixed up."

The door swung open and the woman came back in, carrying a plastic box of various things. "I didn't want to take him into the clinic because his mother is there. It'll break my heart to hear him wail."

"I thought vets were tough."

"Mostly," she said. An Amazon, a solid five-ten, with big hands and a direct gaze. He liked her braid, thick as his forearm and the rich earthen color of a Kauri tree, and her wide, sensual mouth, which belied the no-nonsense attitude she put forth.

He liked her, but she was a bit bound up, wasn't she. He grinned to himself. Make no mistake, beneath the facade was a passionate woman waiting to get out. "You can put him down for a minute," she said. "Let me clean up the wound."

He obliged, leaving his hand close by for the pup to lick as she efficiently but gently cleaned the wound.

"It doesn't need stitches," she said, "which is good." Her mouth turned down, and again he had the sense that she was blinking back tears. "His mama took the bullet for him."

"Bastards."

Her gaze flew up to his. "Exactly."

She had long eyelashes, very dark eyes, angles to the bones of her face that made her look exotic. "You don't look anything like your sister," he commented, thinking of the delicately made, blond Juliet Rousseau.

Her face shuttered. "So I've been told."

Oops, he thought, and filed that away. Couldn't be easy to have a sister who looked exactly like a Barbie doll. "Just an observation, love."

She nodded curtly, and took a bottle from the basket. Shook it briskly. "How do you know Juliet?"

"Josh Mad Calf is a friend of mine."

"Is he? Mine, too." She tested the temperature of the bottle against her inner wrist. "He's a good guy."

"Yeah?" Tam held out his hand. "Don't think I've introduced myself. Tamati Neville. You can call me Tam."

"Desi." She took the hand, shook, let it go. All very efficient. "Tam. The New Zealander. Everyone talks about you. All the women, anyway."

"Yeah?" He grinned. Slowly.

Desi looked weary. "Do me a favor. Save the charm for somebody else. I'm not charmable."

He raised an eyebrow. A challenge he couldn't possibly resist. "That sounds like throwing down a gauntlet to me."

"Trust me," she said, rocking back on her heels. "It's not."

Tam smiled, ever so slightly. "All right. No problem."

"Do you want to feed him?"

He nodded. "I do."

She gave him a bottle. "Have at it. I'm going to see about where to put him to sleep."

"Outside?"

"He's been outside since he was born."

"With his mum!"

She took a breath. "Look, you're thinking Disney. He's a wild animal. I hope we can teach him how to be one."

"Like *Born Free?*"

Desdemona grinned. "Something like that." She snapped her fingers. "I just thought of something. You feed the pup. I'll be back in a few minutes."

Chapter 2

Desi had started the wolf rescue five years ago, when, over the course of a few months, three wolf mixes had been brought to her in various states of despair or disaster, each one the victim of humans not realizing that the wild, free nature of a wolf was not that of a pet. She now offered refuge to a baker's dozen wolves or mixes who had nowhere else to go, and she provided some healing relief for a few, like the pup, who were out of the wild. Others were rescued from a variety of situations, like the female Desi sought now.

In a kennel made warmer by a layer of hay in one corner, Desi found Fir. The dark gray female huddled in one corner, tail draped over her nose.

"Hey, baby," Desi murmured.

The wolf lifted her nose, blinked and with a sigh put her head back down.

The young female had been abandoned by her owner and arrived at the center two months ago, starving. Pregnant. Maladjusted by nature to living in a home with a family, and untrained to survive on her own in the wild, Fir embodied everything that was wrong with humans breeding wolf "dogs." They were not pets. They were not domestic. They did not thrive in homes and towns, or even on ranches. They belonged in the wild, in packs.

Period.

A Gunnison animal control officer had recognized that Fir was a wolf and pregnant, and brought her to Desi, who chose not to terminate the wolf's pregnancy when she was in such poor health. But—perhaps it was regular food, a warm place to sleep, even the hormones coursing through her—Fir seemed to rally, warily joining the firmly established pack, if only at the edges.

Then a month ago her litter had been born, and they'd failed to thrive. Not surprising, given the terrible shape of the mother. Desi had been relieved. The pups were a pit bull-wolf mix, and would only have faced a life of hostility and opposition, completely unsuited to life in a world where their hunting instincts were so thoroughly thwarted or worse, misused.

Fir had not done well since losing her pups. She wouldn't eat. Wouldn't bond with any other creatures, canine or human, wouldn't take care of herself. Her milk was likely dried, but Desi wondered if the

new cub might be a good way to bring Fir back to
the world of the living. Maybe if the cub suckled, the
milk would come.

It was worth a try. She knelt and held out her
hands for the she-wolf to smell. Fir perked up a moment, carefully reading the scent story on Desi's
hands and jeans. She gave Desi's hand a short lick.
"All right, then," she said aloud, rubbing the animal's
ears for a moment. "Let's see what you think of a
baby who isn't yours."

She jogged back to the cabin and flung open the
door—and halted. In spite of herself, she grinned.
Hard to resist that picture. The pup had fallen sound-
ly, deeply asleep against Tam's smooth belly, and
the very faint sound of a snore came from him.

Tam grinned at her. "I can tame even a savage
beast," he said with a quick wink.

The pup was adorable, all round head and paws.
His fur was dark, mottled with the red that would
eventually appear. "He is *very* cute, I have to say."
She gestured. "Bring him out. Let's introduce him to
a possible new mother, see how she does."

"Won't she hurt him?"

Desi shook her head. "Doubtful. We'll stick
around and see what her body language tells us. But
he's a baby. It should be all right."

Tam stood up and followed her out. The wolves
paced along the fences curiously, eyes watching them,
gold and brown and even some blue. There were red
wolves, gray wolves, white and black. Some were
full wolf, others mixed with a wide variety of dog

breeds. The undercoat of many of them was starting to molt out, and the tufts fluttered on the breeze.

None of them spoke, though several lifted their noses to the air, trying to see who had come into their midst.

Next to her, Tam paused in respect. "They're fantastic. Where do they come from?"

"All over. Some puppy mills, some well-meaning people who didn't realize they got a wolf instead of a husky mix." She lifted the catch on the gate that led to an open-air hallway between kennels. To the left was the common area where the animals spent most of their time. It was several heavily fenced acres, forested and rocky, even some natural springs. Individual kennels, each with a cavelike shelter and straw on the ground, housed pairs of wolves at night.

"He's our alpha." Desi pointed to a tall, long-legged male, with a bluish tint to his coat and a brilliant white chest. His hide was crisscrossed with old wounds. "He was a rescue from the dog fights. We get a lot of rescues out of New Mexico here."

"Dog fights? Hard to believe such things still exist."

Desi wondered if he knew he held the pup more closely to his chest. "It's barbaric," she agreed, "but I assure you it still exists."

"I'd kill them if I saw it," he said, and his jaw lifted in a way that made her know he meant it.

"I'd help you." Waving him through in front of her, she closed the gate, and headed beneath a roofed area. "Here's Fir."

The wolf lifted her head as they came in, and Desi

took the pup from Tam, his body relaxed from food and comfort. As Desi took him, however, he jolted into wakefulness and made a series of whimpering, whining noises.

Fir's head lifted urgently, and she sniffed the air. She didn't quite stand up and come rushing over, but it was a good sign, nonetheless. "What do you think, Fir? I brought you a son if you want him."

Gingerly Desi moved closer, keeping her body at the ready in case Fir decided that she'd rather kill him than nurture him. She doubted it, but better to be safe than sorry.

Fir nosed the baby, head to toe, checking ears, rear end, belly, paws. The pup endured it, making mewling sounds. Desi put the baby down and stepped back. "Now we see."

The pup, awkward limbs and plump belly, held his head low, as if waiting for permission. A soft, constant whimper came from him, the low misery of a child who had no hope of relief.

Tam swore, putting his hands beneath his underarms. "It's killing me to watch."

Fir finished her inspection and slumped back to her depressed, half-sleeping, half-staring posture. The pup crawled close beneath her foreleg, and sniffed a teat. With a noise, he plopped down and took the teat in his mouth, and Fir did not object. She didn't nuzzle the baby, but she didn't push him away.

"Good enough," Desi said. The knot that had been lying in her chest all morning eased away. "Let's leave them alone."

They walked back to the driveway. Desi noticed a faint limp. "Did you hurt yourself?"

"Eh? No. Not today. I've got a bum knee."

"And you snowshoe?"

His grin was somewhat sheepish. "Crazy, but I can't stand to be still. Better in the long run, yeah?"

"Probably."

As they reached his car, Tam pulled keys from his pocket. "Do you need anything for him?"

"No, he'll be fine." She tucked her hands in the back pockets of her jeans, trying not to stare too much at his chest, which looked carved and polished into some ideal of perfection of what a man's chest should be. She suppressed an urge to poke him to see if the muscles were as hard as they looked. "You saved his life, you know." She touched her diaphragm, where the sadness had been knotted. "And it made me feel a lot better, too, after losing his mother."

He stood by his car, looking back toward the kennels. "I run a pub," he said, and fixed those pale green eyes on her, so startling in his dark face. "Would it be any help to you to bring the expired meats we can't use?"

"Yes! Please! It's always hard to get enough meat for them."

"Will do."

"And if you or any of your buddies have leftover game meat, all the better. It's that time of year that people clean out their freezers for the summer fishing season."

"I'll spread the word," he said with a nod. He

stuck out his big hand. "Nice to meet you, Dr. Rousseau. Come in the pub and I'll buy you lunch and a beer."

"Call me Desi," she said, and put her hand in his. Was it her imagination, or did a little spark zap her palm? "And, thanks, but I don't drink."

"Nothing?"

"Not alcohol."

"I've got beer from twenty-two countries," he said with an absolutely charming tilt of his grin. "But hot chocolate from England, too, and some sodas from Australia. Or…hmm. Ever tried an Irn Bru? Scottish, not too sweet."

Desi realized she was falling right under the spell of that grin. "I'm sure it's delicious." She tugged her hand away, took a step backward. His grin expanded the slightest bit. "I've got to get to work now."

"All right, then." He waved. "I'll be back."

With a nod Desi turned away, trying to calm the little leap of hope those words gave her. Hadn't she learned anything? Charming men were as deep as a rain puddle.

Not to mention he was way out of her league. Men like that loved women like her sisters—the soft, sweet blonde or the fiery redhead—not serious-minded, solid brunettes with cracked cuticles. She'd let down her guard to allow Claude in, and look where it had landed her.

She headed for the kennels. A good romp with the pack would lift her spirits and wash the man right out of her mind. Wolves were loyal beings, after all. Men could take a lesson from them.

Still, she couldn't help looking over her shoulder as his car headed up the road. As men went, he was a pretty spectacular specimen.

And alpha. Definitely alpha, though he would pretend to be the playful beta, second in command.

Don't even think about it, she told herself again. Don't. Even. Think. About. It.

By the end of the week the pup and Fir seemed to be making a fine recovery. When she checked on them Thursday, the pup was even nursing as if he was getting nourishment. Desi left them alone and carried her paperwork home to finish a grant proposal to gain funds from an outdoor wildlife foundation.

Friday morning she awakened to find an especially large pile of dogs sleeping in front of the pot-bellied stove. For a long moment, she peered at them, trying to figure out what they'd done to make themselves look like such a big pile.

Then the reality crystallized: in addition to her own dogs, there were three wolves from the pack sleeping in a tangle on the floor.

In the house.

She peered at them in confusion, trying to figure out how—

Suddenly she sprang to her feet, thinking of the rest of the wolves, running free in the forest—and across ranch land where lots of tasty tidbits of sheep and chicken roamed.

"Crap," she muttered under her breath and shoved

legs into jeans, a sweater over the sleeveless T-shirt she'd slept in, and some socks and shoes on her feet.

The wolves and dogs roused themselves, greeting her, each according to his or her nature. A lick, a polite, patient gaze, a leap toward her belly. "Okay, okay, okay!" she cried, petting heads, chests; tugging Tecumseh's ear, letting Aladdin slurp her wrist. "We gotta go, gang." She gave her special whistle, and they all leaped up and ran outside, waiting while she locked the door to the cabin.

Then they all ran up the hill in a pack, some streaking ahead at point, two lagging in the rear to make sure the flank was protected. They dashed under tree branches and dove around rocks, tails high as feathers in the Colorado morning.

All the way there, Desi prayed it was not what she feared, that the other wolves would be safe and sound when she got there. And if the fence *had* been compromised for some reason, that no one else had gotten out.

Her mind raced. Even if the fence was down, the wolves should have been in their kennels overnight— protected with a double layer of fencing. She ran harder, wishing she'd taken some time to put on a bra to keep everything in place. But there was no time to change things now.

When she reached the kennel, she rounded the free-running pack and directed them into an area they used to isolate new animals or those with a problem of some kind. It was double fenced, with a small circumference of fencing around the outside of it, but she gave it the once-over anyway, and saw that it was fine.

Closing the dogs in the area to keep them safe, she dashed to the cabin and banged on the door to wake up her assistant, Alex. "Need you out here, man!" she cried, and headed for the external fencing to see where the problem was.

The area was fenced to a distance of several acres, but Desi didn't have to go that far to find the hole.

The fence was cut. Cleanly and professionally, with wire cutters. It was big enough for Desi to walk through, never mind the wolves. She stood there in the early morning light, fist clenched, afraid to go check the kennels to see who was here and who was not, terrified that the others might have been poisoned with bad meat or worse.

Alex rushed out, his hair sticking up, his feet bare. "What the hell happened?"

She shook her head. "Somebody obviously cut it." Roughly she said, "Help me check the wolves. Three of them were asleep in my living room this morning. Let's see if anybody else got out."

With relief, they discovered most of the wolves were still safely penned in their kennels, Naomi and Hercules together in a pile; Caesar, Simon and Ralph in another kennel.

But when she got to Fir's kennel, Desi's heart plummeted. The gate stood open, plainly just propped open and left that way. The lost, lonely, heartsore wolf was gone, no doubt to continue her quest to find her master, the bastard who'd abandoned her so completely.

Huddled in the corner, hidden by the shadows, was the pup.

Desi cursed loudly and picked up the sleeping pup, who did not appear to have come through the night with any damage, and put him in Alex's waiting arms. "Get him into the clinic and give him some ground venison, and call Linda to see if she can come in early to give you a hand. I'll see if I can track Fir before she gets far."

Alex bent his body protectively around the pup. "What are we going to do about the fence?"

"Fix it." She flung her braid over her shoulder and felt it thump hard against her left shoulder blade. "The wolves will just have to stay in their kennels today." She scowled, feeling fury rise like lava through her chest. "Bastards."

"Go find her."

Desi bent to examine the area around Fir's kennel. It was hard to pick out the wolf's track amid the footprints in the passageway, but she found the tracks easily in the deep snow beneath the trees in the forest, a trail of paws headed directly for the woods. Uphill, of course.

A warm stretch had begun melting the sunny spots on the southern-facing slope, and twice Desi lost the trail, then picked it up again after a few feet. A tuft of molting undercoat was caught on a crooked branch close to the ground, and Desi tugged it off. Fir was trotting at a pretty quick pace. Hunting, perhaps, on the trail of some scent.

Suddenly the trail disappeared, as if the wolf

had vanished, tucked inside a magic rock, or been beamed out of there by means of a transporter. Intellectually Desi knew the trail had not just ended, that she as tracker had simply failed, and she traced backward, then in a meticulous circle. When that failed to yield the track, Desi stopped and looked around carefully for the possibility of a den. A cave, a hole in the ground, a hidden place behind another trunk. Something.

But there were only trees and the piles of pine needles on the ground, and snow in drifts and clusters of ice-covered rocks. No sign at all of Fir. Desi dropped her hands in frustration.

"Fir!" she cried, and gave her special whistle. In the distance, a bird whistled back. It sounded forlorn.

Helplessly, she scanned the area, thinking of the poor lost wolf, her faithful, hopeless quest and the baby who might have had a mother and now would not. All because someone had cut the fence. Who would *do* something so evil?

Whoever it was, Desi thought, she was going to make damned sure they were caught and punished. Enough was enough. If her enemies wanted a war, she'd give them a war.

But first things first. She had to get to town and order some new fencing, then file a complaint with the police.

Tam loved many things, small to large. Hot showers after a cold run. His sister in New Zealand, who worked as a nurse in an Auckland hospital. A cup of chocolate. The sight of a woman's bare back, curving down to her bottom. Rugby—both playing and watching. His pub, the Black Crown, of which he was so proud that his mother—had she lived—would have scolded him for tempting the gods.

The Black Crown occupied a building that had been serving libations to Mariposans as far back as the gold rush, though it had been called Molly's Tavern for most of that time. Tam had bought it a little more than two years before and renovated it into a classic British-style pub that specialized in beers from around the world and old-fashioned pub food like hamburgers and shepherd's pie and even a ploughman's platter with cheeses and pickles, all foods that were very big with the Europeans who came to Mariposa to hike and ski. He'd done well.

In general, his easy-going nature made running the pub a fairly straightforward undertaking. As a rule, Tam was not easily annoyed. Life was too short to spend it grousing and whining. May as well get on with things, make life work as it was, rather than trying to make it something else.

But anyone who worked for him knew he was a fanatic about cleanliness, a lesson learned at his grandfather's diner. The Shark and Tatie had been a shack on the edge of the road toward the Bay of Islands that served fish so fresh it had been swimming hours before, along with piles of roasted kumara and thick, hot chips to tourists driving up to see the grand rocks off the coast.

A restaurant, his grandfather taught him, could

never be too clean. Tam had fired more employees over sloppy cleaning than over being late.

And this morning, as he remopped the bar floor that had not been done well enough last night, he knew there was going to be one more. Not that he was pleased about it. Help was hard to find, and the competition for every pair of hands was steep in the tourist economy of Mariposa. This was his third winter here, and he'd grown to recognize the signs of ski bums ready to head west for surfing or into the city for real jobs now that the season was nearly spent. Kaleb, the boy Tam would have to fire, loved only skiing. He'd dropped out of college to ski. He was a great bartender, a decent short-order cook, and Tam hated to let him go, but the kitchen looked as if it hadn't even been touched this morning.

His day cook, a skinny man with a Fu Manchu mustache, was furious. "You gotta get on the night crew, man," he said. "I can't work like this. It's crap."

"I hear you, mate. It's done."

The lunch crowd would be arriving within minutes, but Tam took the chance to give the place a good scrubbing down—the grill and the walls, the far dark corners of the old kitchen, the shelves where the heavy pots lived. He took everything out of the walk-in fridge and washed down the shelves with bleach water, taking inventory as he went. Brown lettuce and a moldy tomato went in the bin, along with freezer-burned ice cream.

And he sorted out meats beyond their due date for the wolves, putting them in a box he marked with a bright green Sharpie: "Don't use. Don't toss. Save for Tam."

When the back was finished, he headed to the front of the house, where the radio played the reggae music the servers liked, and got ready to open for lunch. The bartender, Alice, a pretty girl with eyes still sleep-swollen, carried a tray filled with freshly wiped-down salt and pepper shakers. "Hey, Tamati," she said, and yawned. "How's your day so far?"

He pulled stools off the old bar and settled them on the wooden floor. "Excellent."

"You always say that," she said, and peered at him. "Don't you ever have a bad morning?"

Tam shook his head. "Nope. Life is too short, babe."

"You got a lot of change in that wolf thingy," she said. "You notice?"

"Ha. No." After finding the wolf pup three days ago, Tam had taken some empty pickle jars and put pictures of wolves on them, and a request that said simply, "Please Help the Wolf Center." Couldn't hurt, anyway.

The door swung open. Tam raised his head. "Sorry. We're not open for another twenty minutes. Can you come back?"

Elsa, his erstwhile girlfriend—not very much of a girlfriend, he admitted only to himself—popped her sunstreaked blond head around the door. Her teeth seemed extra big and white in her tanned face as she grinned at him. "Surprise!" She held up a brightly colored bag. "I brought you a present from Jamaica."

Alice had been waiting for direction, and he

nodded. "Hello, Elsa." He let her kiss his cheek. "How was the honeymoon?"

She glided into the room, three full feet of legs, the rest hair, bust and eyes the clear, unreal color of blue curaçao. "Wonderful!" Her Swedish accent added the last, completely unnecessary dash. "We snorkeled and swam and sunned." She held out a graceful forearm. "You see? I am your color now!"

Tam realized that somehow, over the past three months, he'd completely recovered from his bizarre infatuation with Elsa Franz—now Biloxi. "Glad to hear it." He took the offered bag and opened it to find a T-shirt, black, with a silly slogan on the front. He didn't wear clothes with words.

"Brilliant. Thanks." He folded the shirt back neatly and tucked it in the bag. "Can I get you something? Coffee?"

"No, no. I will have to be going." She caught sight of the solicitation jar and scowled. Pulling it close to peer at the photo, she asked, "Is this the wolf center up on the gate road?"

"The very one."

She shook her head. "You should not raise money for her! She's a murderer. Haven't you heard the story?"

"She's no murderer." Tam shook his head, wiped the bar. "No more than you."

Elsa's eyes widened, the thick mascara seeming somehow ridiculous in this environment. "She did! She killed her husband, Claude. The Indian artist."

He looked her in the eye. Raised a brow.

Her hands fluttered. "Well, you still shouldn't be

supporting the wolf center." She inclined a shoulder, bent in confidentially. "Bill and I bought the land right next to it, and he's given me carte blanche to develop it into a spa! There are mineral waters—hot springs!—and we've already hired an architect to design and build it."

"And where will the wolves go, eh?"

"The land is too valuable for that kind of use. She can find a better place where there is not so much skiing and desire to build homes."

For one split second, he felt a flash of anger. He was conscious of his nostrils flaring. "They were here first," he said.

Elsa's expression shifted. She reached for his hand, curled her cold fingers around his wrist. "I apologize, Tamati. I forget how indigenous people feel about the animals."

He removed his arm from her grip. "I have work to do," he said.

"Ah, Tamati," she said with a sigh. "I did not mean to offend you. I am sorry."

"Don't worry," he said stiffly. "You know me. Never angry."

Uncertainty clouded her eyes. She searched his face, then stood. "Okay. I do not want to make you angry with me." She headed for the door. "Bye-bye."

"Bye." When she had closed the door behind her, Tam allowed himself a low, furious growl. Honestly, what had he ever seen in such a shallow, social-climbing—

Never mind. What was done was done.

But he wondered if Desi knew about the spa and the hot springs. He smiled to himself, turning the solicitation jar toward the front of the house. Under his breath he whistled a happy little tune.

Chapter 3

By the time she hit town, Desi was coldly, furiously focused. She had gone back to the cabin, grabbed her keys off the counter and jumped in her truck. She had not had coffee or breakfast or taken time to do anything but let down her braid and comb it out.

Just as she parked at the hardware store, her veterinary cell phone, clipped to her hip, rang loudly. "Dr. Rousseau," she snapped into the receiver.

"Good morning, Desdemona," said a full, drawling voice. "How are you?"

"Hey, Judge!" Desi unbuckled her seat belt and took a moment. Alexander Yancy, a farmer who'd made his fortune in the organic market, focusing on free-range chickens, pigs and cows, was a good friend. He'd proved instrumental in helping to get her released on bond when she had been arrested for Claude's murder. "Hey, Judge. I've had better days, but I've had worse. How are you?"

"I'm all right," he said, "but Lacey's had better days." Lacey was his horse, a youthful and high spirited mare who was always getting in some kind of trouble. "I was hoping you might have a chance to come look at her."

"What's wrong?"

"She's just lethargic. Not overly sick that I can see, and I can't see any injury, but she's not herself."

Desi sensed there was more to it than the judge was saying. That maybe it wasn't about the horse at all. She smiled gently. The judge had been unexpectedly widowed four years ago, and he'd taken to Desi as if she were a long-lost daughter. "I have a few things to do this morning in town," she said. "What if I try to stop by after lunch?"

"I could make you some lunch if you'd like. Apple walnut salad? Made with my very own harvest, though I must admit they're getting somewhat mealy now."

She smiled, hoping the expression translated down the phone wires. "I'd love to, Judge, but somebody cut my fencing and I've got a heck of a lot to do today. How about later this week?"

"That's fine, girl. You do what you need to do."

"I will stop by and see Lacey on my way home."

"I'll keep the coffeepot warm."

Desi hung up, feeling less furious. Thank heaven for Alexander Yancy, she thought, heading into the hardware store. She wasn't sure what she would have done without him when she was arrested three months ago. His help had been instrumental in securing bail and getting the insubstantial charges knocked down to the current level.

Inside the hardware store, she ordered the fencing she needed and arranged for it to be delivered. The man in the lumber area seemed as if he might have wanted to deliver the next day, seeing as it was nearly eleven o'clock, but something about the bristling fury in Desi's attitude made him back off. "It'll be there by two."

"Better be," she said, "or I swear, John, I'll be back down here raising hell."

The older man half grinned, his face a mass of sun lines in a leathery mask. "Hell, darlin', seeing you in such a fine snit, it'd almost be worth it."

"Don't make me come back down here. The wolves need to be safe."

As she strode back to her truck, he called out behind her, "Your hair sure looks purty like that!"

Desi heard the teasing admiration in his voice and waved without turning around. She slammed the door closed and fired up the engine, feeling a deep sense of satisfaction as she guided the enormous vehicle out of the lot, the engine rumbling and powerful. It was a working truck, with a water tank that fit in the bed, and the power to haul whatever she needed up the mountain, along with four-wheel drive and clearance enough to navigate the worst pot holes in the dirt road to the cabin.

But all that said, she just liked it. Loved the way she felt driving it, with her big hands and long legs. It made her feel powerful.

It was not, however, a great vehicle for driving through town during the height of ski season, especially through the heavily pedestrian areas of downtown. It was too aggravating. She parked in a lot within walking distance of all the places she needed to visit and locked up.

Walking, however, did not cool her temper. When she hit the front desk of the sheriff's office, she was in what her father would have called Full Desi Outrage. "I need to talk to somebody about some harassment on my land," she said.

The woman behind the desk nodded. "It's okay. I'll be glad to get somebody to take your complaint—"

"I've got it," said a man coming in from a back room, papers in his hand.

Desi looked up. It was Gene Nordquist, the young, power-mad deputy who had made her life a living hell the past six months. "No," Desi said, brooking no argument. "He's not objective. He's been giving me grief all the time lately. Somebody else."

The woman half shrugged. "There's not anybody else, not unless you want to come back later."

Desi spun her on her heel, the lava rising in her throat. "Damned right I'll come back."

Furious, stinging, she stomped off through the snow toward her sister's house. Juliet had rented a house in downtown Mariposa to be close by to her fiancé, Josh. The two were planning a summer wedding, but everyone wanted to wait until the business with Claude's murder was finished.

If it was *ever* finished, Desi thought with some despair. She had really expected it to be cleared up by now. Now the wolves were being made to pay, and she would not allow that to happen. If the police would not help her find out who was harassing her, she'd find out on her own. If they refused to find out who killed Claude, Desi would do it herself.

But how? Desi needed Juliet's and Josh's expertise. Juliet was a lawyer. Josh was a tribal policeman, and had officially taken himself off the case. She knew he couldn't ethically do anything to compromise his position, but that didn't mean he couldn't help her brainstorm.

And, heck, it had been ages since she'd seen Glory, Josh's five-year-old daughter. It would be refreshing, cheering, to have the little girl's company. Everyone should be around on a Saturday morning. She looked at her watch and was amazed to realize it was nearly lunchtime. That would account for the grumbling in her stomach. She hadn't even had breakfast.

Leaving the truck parked, she walked to Juliet's cottage and knocked. Jack, Josh's fluffy dog, who now only stayed at Juliet's house, jumped up in the window and wagged his tail, but there was obviously no one else at home. Disappointed, Desi pulled out her cell phone and dialed her sister's number.

Juliet picked up on the second ring. "Hi, Dez. Where are you?"

"I'm on your front porch teasing your dog. Where are you?"

"I'm having lunch at the Black Crown. Come join me."

"The Black Crown?"

"Yeah, the New Zealander's pub. It's great food. You'll like it."

Something purply and yearning burst in Desi's belly. She looked down at her careless attire, the jeans and quickly donned sweater, her muddy boots and loose hair. "Ooh, I can't! I look terrible. It's been a horrible morning."

"First of all you never look terrible, and second, what happened?"

Desi felt the weight of the lost wolf, the cut fence, in the tight muscles over her shoulders. "Long story," she said, and the sound of it must have been in her voice.

"Desi, please come eat with me. I haven't seen you in more than a week. I'll ask the server for a paper bag you can put over your head. How's that?"

Desi loved her sister, but the woman was a beauty and always had been. "Is the owner there?" she asked.

"Tam? Yeah. I'm looking right at him." She paused. "Why?"

Desi sighed. "No reason."

"Do you know him?"

"Not really. He found a wolf cub and brought it to the center the other day." And then she realized her sister might think she was attracted to Tam. "Seems to think pretty well of himself, doesn't he?"

"You didn't like him?"

Desi shrugged, walking down the sidewalk in the sunshine, feeling her spirits lighten the smallest bit. "I didn't say that. He seemed nice enough. Maybe it's just the whole Claude thing—I don't trust charming men."

Juliet chuckled. "It's possible to be charming and a good guy at the same time."

"Maybe. But not charming, drop dead gorgeous *and* a nice guy."

"I didn't say nice guy," Juliet said. "I said good guy. Not necessarily the same thing at all."

"Whatever." Desi turned the corner and realized that her feet had taken her right down to the pub. Her heart fluttered painfully as she stood across the street, cars thickly moving by in an endless stream. Her sister was on the phone, sitting in the window of the pub beneath a cleverly painted logo. Juliet's blond hair shone like soft wheat in the sunlight and her curvy figure was draped in a thick red sweater that showed a generous amount of cleavage.

"You look very pretty today," Desi said, and when Juliet looked out the window, she grinned.

Juliet waved her inside. "Come in and have lunch!"

"I will have to cross the street to get there."

"Not always the easiest task," Juliet said with a chuckle. "Of course, you could go to the corner and cross with the light."

"Lights are for sissies." Desi stood a moment longer, letting cars swish by on the street. What if Tam thought she was chasing him or something? They'd never met before and she'd never been to the pub, now they'd met and here she was? She had no illusions. She was not in his league. Not at all.

Which, she thought with sudden enlightenment, she should take as a good thing and quite protective. Especially considering she had not a scrap of makeup on and her clothes were old and worn. With a slight smile, she waited for a break in traffic and dashed across the street.

Tam was ringing up a ticket when the door swung open and Desi Rousseau tumbled inside, blinking like a wild animal come out of the woods. A bolt of sharp, hot awareness zoomed through his body, nape to tailbone, and didn't stop there. It moved down— femur to knee to arches of his feet.

He realized he was staring and turned his attention to the ticket in his hands, but the pleasure at her arrival was still there. He gave the server her ticket, filled glasses with soda and lime, wiped off the bar, all the while sneaking glances, pretending not to notice.

Not his type. In a way she reminded him of a sturdy Maori woman, strong and healthy, with lots of curves and strong hands and a no-nonsense way of walking. He tended to go for wistful-looking women, like her sister sitting there in a pool of sunlight with her blond head.

He frowned. He found himself standing straighter, gathering details about Desi as she settled in. She was absolutely unadorned. A wide brow and large dark eyes, a tumble of thick, very long hair.

And maybe braless. He shouldn't be noticing,

should he, but he was a man, and there was all that luscious, swaying movement. Healthy, high breasts above a narrow waist and rolling hips in a pair of jeans worn to a pale white softness.

Not his type, but there he was, walking across the room. "Hello!" he said, as she sat down. "How are you?"

"Not bad," Desi said, settling in the booth. She gave him a cursory glance. Or what was meant to be cursory. She couldn't hide the slight flush on her neck, the faint flare of her nostrils, and probably didn't even realize her gaze slid down to his mouth, that she touched her hair, her cheek, then her waist.

Still, she gave nonchalance a shot. "Tam, right?"

He smiled, very slowly. "That's right. And you're…" he tried to think how to get her name wrong "…Desiree?"

"It's Desi. Short for Desdemona."

"Ah. Right." He nodded. "Good to have you in my pub. Can I bring you something to drink, cuz?"

"Please. I haven't had a thing. I need coffee. Coffee and cream and tons of sugar. Please." She looked at him. "And what is your best dish, Tam?"

For one long moment their eyes locked. He saw beyond the facade, the nervousness, to the natural woman within her. He saw, in that split second, looking into the depths of her velvety, wild-woman eyes, that *she* didn't know it—and he was sure it was probably a bad idea—but eventually, they were going to have very, very hot sex.

He sincerely hoped it was sooner rather than later.

He blinked, slowly, and touched his tongue to his lower lip. "I'll surprise you, shall I?"

The dimple deep in her left cheek flashed. "That sounds just fine."

Again he felt that bolt of awareness shoot through him. Round his ribs, slamming into palms that wanted to rub themselves across her skin, needling alive other parts of him. "Be right back."

He swung away and headed to the back room, surprised. *Whew*. What was that about?

Ducking into the kitchen, he turned and glanced back out through the circle window in the door. The woman leaned over the table, her magnificent hair catching sunlight, glinting gold and copper. He could tell by their posture that Juliet was admonishing Desi, and Desi was blowing her off.

"Give me a hefty plate of the roast lamb," he said, then hesitated. It was a house specialty, a stew made from his own grandmother's recipe, and a huge favorite among the hikers and skiers.

But a lot of Americans didn't like lamb, had never really eaten it much. He held up a hand. "Wait a minute." He poured a cup of coffee, filled a pitcher with cream and carried it to the sisters' table. "Here you go, love," he said, putting a little spin on the pitcher.

"Wonderful!"

"I was going to bring you out our house specialty," he said, "but thought I should ask if you eat lamb."

Juliet leaned forward. "Yes," she said. "You really have to try it. There's nothing like it. And roast potatoes."

"Oh, like I need roast potatoes!" Desi said with a scowl.

"Nothing wrong with all those curves," he said, and winked.

She shook her head. "Didn't we already have this discussion about trying to charm me?"

He laughed. "I'll be right back."

Desi was charmed. It was impossible not to be. That wide grin, the twinkle in his eye, the sense of broad good humor.

Juliet noticed. "It might be a little soon, sis."

"Soon for what?"

"Another man. A new guy. Claude has only been dead three months."

"Our marriage was dead quite a while before that." Desi stirred cream into her coffee, watching the swirl rise in curlicues from the bottom, turning the mixture exactly the color of Tam's skin. "He's way out of my league, anyway," she said, and took a sip too fast. The hot coffee burned her tongue. "And, even if that were not true, I would not need my little sister to tell me when to get involved with somebody."

"Ooh, prickly!" Her blue eyes flashed. "You *must* like him!"

Out of the corner of her eye, she saw him returning with two plates. "Here he comes. Please stop. Don't embarrass me."

"I would never!"

With a flourish, he put a slice of quiche and some roasted orange vegetable in front of Juliet, and a steaming pile of meat and vegetables in front of Desi. Her stomach growled at the beauty of it. "Wow. This seems pretty fancy for a pub."

"We aim to please," he said. "Can I join you, girls?"

"Of course." Juliet scooted over toward the window. "Come sit by me."

"Sure?" he said, sliding in. "I don't want Josh punching my eye out, now." He grinned at Desi over the table, his pale green eyes direct and almost too probing.

And for a moment she was lost in the look of him, the high cheekbones, the alluring shadow on his jaw, his wide mouth. She could smell him, strongly, very specifically, a hint of cinnamon and morning sun. His eyes were extraordinary, the pale green of new pine needles, so unusual in his dark face.

Food, she told herself. *Eat.* She picked up her fork.

The meat was hot, tender, exquisitely perfect. "Oh, my gosh," she said after the first bite, and took another. "Oh, that is so good!"

"Toldja," Juliet said, nodding. "Tam learned to cook at his grandmother's knee, isn't that right?"

He nodded. "My grandfather had a restaurant on the tourist road to Cape Reinga. They put me to work very early."

"What's Cape Reinga?" Desi asked. She wanted him to keep talking, so she could keep eating. She wasn't sure if it was the fact that she'd skipped breakfast, or that the food was just simply spectacular, but she hadn't tasted anything so delicious in ages.

"The northernmost point of New Zealand," Tam

said. "The Pacific and the Tasman Sea meet there. It's beautiful."

"I'd love visit New Zealand," Desi said.

"It's a beautiful place."

"So why are you here instead of there?"

"I was a rugby player, once upon a time," he said, pointing out the jerseys on the wall, lifting an eyebrow. "When I got cut, I looked around for something to do, and I took up smoke jumping."

Desi laughed. "Just a little sideline, huh?"

"Something to do while I saw the world." He shrugged. "I had a thing for explorers when I was a kid. I wanted to—" he used his big, graceful hand to illustrate in the air "—circumnavigate the globe, like Magellan."

Desi blinked, the food forgotten in front of her. "No way."

Juliet laughed, slapping Tam's shoulder. "I think you might need to let me out. I'm sure I can't stand to be stuck here with two explorer geeks."

Tam's face brightened. "Did you like explorers, too?"

"'Like' is an understatement," Juliet said, despite the look Desi shot her. "She had an actual picture of Marco Polo on her bedroom wall. You know, like where most girls would hang a picture of a rock star or something?"

Embarrassed, Desi kicked her sister under the table, and got Tam instead. He laughed and covered her hand with both of his. "Don't be embarrassed! When you're finished here, you have to come see my apartment."

"To see your etchings?"

"To see my maps." He wiggled his eyebrows. "I have the maps of Magellan, Vespucci and Marco Polo on the wall—and there are others in my files. I just haven't had them framed yet."

Desi grinned. She couldn't help it. "I do want to see them!" She took a bite of the lamb. "After I eat."

"Who is your favorite?"

Spearing a perfect medallion of carrot, she narrowed her eyes. "I don't know. Cook was pretty interesting, with the diet stuff. But one hates to say that to a Maori."

He chuckled. "They were all bastards if you want to look at it from the perspective of the indigenous people."

"Wait," Juliet said. "Captain Cook is a real person?"

"He is," Tam said. "Discovered New Zealand and Tahiti and Hawaii."

"And got conked over the head and died in a Native fight," Desi added.

"Which is also pretty much how Magellan died," Tam said.

"I need to get out of here," Juliet said. "*Age of Explorers* left me dead asleep."

Tam met Desi's eyes across the table, and there was a distinct, powerful zing. Scary. Thrilling. Exciting.

"An adventure," he said. Quietly.

"But how," Desi asked, "did you end up in *Mariposa?* It's a little out of the way."

"Hayman fire." It had been an enormous fire that devoured millions of acres of Colorado forest a few

years before. "I had a bad landing and busted up my
leg, so I spent a bit of time recovering around here."
His gaze shifted toward the window, to the craggy
San Juans visible against the cerulean sky. "Something about this place just grabbed me."

"The Mariposa claim," Desi said, grinning herself.
"They say the Lady of the Shrine calls certain people
to the area."

"Yeah? I haven't heard that one."

Desi looked away from the jutting angle of his
Adam's apple in a strong throat. *Don't want it,* she
told herself. *Don't want anything.* "She must have
called you."

"Something did, that's sure." He shifted direction.
"How's the pup?"

"Pup?" Juliet asked.

"Tam found a wolf cub." The whole morning
crashed back into her world. "He's okay," she said.
"But Fir—the surrogate mother—she escaped. I
don't know where she is."

"Oh, no!" Juliet cried. She'd had a special affinity
with the fearful she-wolf. "What happened?"

So Desi recounted the miserable story of her
morning, ending with the encounter at the sheriff's
office. "I've got to get someone more sympathetic up
there to look around before all the evidence is gone,"
she said, "but if I have to, I'll live with Nordquist."

"Who would *do* that?" Juliet asked. "I mean, it's
so bad for the ranchers and the tourists and everybody else to have the wolves wandering around."

"Most of them won't go anywhere," Desi said.

"They've been around long enough they'll just stay there. So it's somebody who doesn't really understand that—or somebody who is just harassing me." She mopped up the last of the gravy with a white roll and sat back with a sigh. "I should feel guilty, but I don't. I have to work on that fence this afternoon."

"You don't have any idea who would do it?" Juliet asked. "Maybe that would help."

"I have ideas. I had another offer from Bill Biloxi, the developer who wants to open a spa next to my land, and I refused it. I guess his girlfriend is pretty upset about it."

"Wife," Tam said. "They got married."

"Ah. You know them?"

"Her."

He didn't elaborate, but Desi picked up a vibe that made her look at him a little more closely. "Well," she said, "they're certainly not the only ones. I've had twelve offers on the land in the past three months, and there's something heating up. I'm not sure what's going on, but it's making me nervous."

"Especially because somebody killed Claude," Juliet said. "As *dangerous* goes, that's pretty high up there."

Desi shrugged. "But it doesn't make sense that someone should have killed him to get to the land. We were divorcing."

"What if they wanted to scare you into selling?"

"I suppose," she said, but her gut said that wasn't it. "I just think Claude finally crossed the wrong person." She spied the clock and saw the hands creeping toward noon. "Damn! I have to get out of here." She took a big gulp of coffee, dabbed her mouth with a napkin, stood up. "They're delivering my fencing at two."

Tam stood with her. "You'll have to come see my maps another time."

"I really will," Desi said, looking up at his face. She hadn't noticed the very small patch of hair he wore beneath his lip, and it gave her a strange, hot buzz of desire. He was taller than she by a few inches, and the solidness of him pleased her. He seemed unmovable.

"I cleaned out the freezers this morning," he said, "and put aside a box of freezer-burned meats. Can I bring them to you later?"

Desi knew she should say no, tell him that she had a lot to do, that maybe he should come another day. He was a distraction she just didn't need right now.

But he regarded her steadily with those pale, waterlike green eyes, his mouth a patient bow. She found herself wondering what it would be like to kiss him, to run the tip of her tongue over that small, exotic patch of beard below his lip.

She swallowed. "Yes," she said. "Please do."

Chapter 4

Back at the police station Desi spied Nordquist driving away, and hurried inside to make her report. With relief she knew she'd be directed to Jimmy Rineheart, a stooped man with a belly round as a bowling ball. His horses were under her care.

"How're you doing, Dr. Rousseau?"

Relieved, she sat down next to the metal desk. "Not great, Jimmy. This mess is driving me crazy. How's Pappy?" Pappy was his gentle, ancient paint, a horse that liked nothing more than to munch hay all day long in a sunny meadow.

"He's fine, fine. 'Bout time for his checkup, I reckon." He tugged out a pencil. "Now what's the trouble today?"

Again Desi outlined the vandalism, and the deputy scribbled notes on an official-looking form. "Obviously," she said, "I've got to get it fixed today so the wolves are safe, but can you take a look, see if you can find out who did this?"

He sighed. "We've been through this with the ravens, honey."

For months, Desi had been finding dead ravens on her land, around the house, even one in her truck once. It had started before Claude died, and she'd believed at first that it was his doing—either trying to scare her or just harass her enough to make her give up the land.

Died. Odd choice of words. Yeah, Claude *died,* all right—from a bullet through his chest.

To the sheriff she said, "I know. But don't you think this seems like a step toward more serious? I'm worried about my wolves."

"It does," he agreed in his slow way. He tapped his pen on his nose for a minute. "Not likely to find a lot, you know."

"I know. Maybe a footprint or something?"

He gave her a wry grin. "Now, we haven't even figured out who killed that worthless husband of yours, have we? If we can't solve a murder, how we gonna solve a vandalism nobody cares about?"

Desi nodded, all the ease engendered by the good meal now leaking out of her body through the soles of her feet, making her feel like a rag doll, depleted and dull.

"Well, thank you," she said, and stood up. "At least I've made a formal complaint."

He tapped the paper. "I've got it all right here, sweetheart. You take care now, you hear?"

"Thanks, Jimmy."

"Don't lose heart. Things work out in the end."

Desi paused. "Do they?" she asked. "I'm not sure."

He looked sad, but what could he do? He was only one part of the law, not the whole thing. Disheartened, she headed back to her truck and drove to the vet clinic to check in with her staff and the small-animals hospitalized there before she headed back up the mountain to meet the delivery.

The clinic was her first, and she was proud of it, a smallish building at the western end of town, neatly painted, with a professional sign standing in front: Rousseau Animal Clinic, All Creatures Large and Small....

A sign currently obscured by a little circle of women with hand-lettered placards on sticks, circling in protest in the parking lot. "Remember Claude Tsosie?" one read and another read, "How Can a Killer Tend Your Animals? Boycott Rousseau Veterinary Clinic."

Desi stamped on the gas and roared into the parking lot, the lava of her anger boiling up to the point of explosion, burning in her throat and ears and chest. She had a blistering vision of slamming her foot down on the gas pedal and mowing the lot of them down.

Instead, she curved the big truck into her parking space and turned it off, slamming the door as hard as she could. It was heavy steel, and it made a satisfying clunk behind her as she marched across the lot. The dentist's wife, a dark-haired woman with giant blue eyes, who'd had a crush on Claude from the moment he arrived in Mariposa, led the group. Probably her meet-and-greet from church, Desi thought darkly, and stormed up to her.

"Get off my property," she said. "Move your little posse over to the sidewalk or I'll call the police."

Alice Turner blinked. Her tight little mouth curled the slightest bit. "The police? The ones who have accused you of Claude's murder, you mean?"

"Get. Off," Desi said, pointing to the sidewalk.

Alice waved a languid hand, and the four women circling the parking lot moved to a sidewalk where Desi had no claim and started circling there, droning some chant.

Idiots! The whole lot of them had been taken in by Claude's charm and his apparent sincerity and modest talents as a painter.

Mostly they'd been taken in by his good looks.

For Claude Tsosie had been a very beautiful man. Not just a little bit handsome, not buff or cute or a hottie. He'd been drop-dead gorgeous, like a painting or a statue, or something conjured up by a woman's fertile imagination. Just over six feet tall, lean and loose limbed, graceful as a hawk, he'd grown out his long, heavy, black hair until it reached his waist. He had twinkling brown eyes and high cheekbones and a beautiful mouth, and long-fingered graceful hands and even a very good voice.

The ultimate female fantasy.

Desi, too, had fallen for it.

Standing in the parking lot, with a load of fencing about to be delivered, and a wolf lost in the woods because of vandals, Desi consciously unclenched her fists. Her anger was a dangerous and volatile thing these days. The lava could burn her, too, if she let it get out of control.

And yet, what else was there to hang on to? Sometimes she was afraid it was the only thing that kept her going.

She dropped off some papers at the clinic, checked messages and headed back up the mountain, dogged by a sense of futility. What was the point of all this struggle? She and Claude had come here to build a life, to make a family, their dreams simple and sweet. Desi sought a place she might finally call home, a place where she could be accepted and loved as herself, at long last. Claude had dreamed of selling his paintings, and wanted to build their home while she built her veterinary practice.

For a time it had gone just that way.

She didn't know when it had gone wrong. Or if it had always been wrong and she was just too smitten to notice, or if he'd gone bad when she started getting busy with the practice or if—

Stop it. There was no point trying to unravel anything in the past. She had to focus on the now. On the future. On taking care of her land and the hot springs, the wolves and the wild natural beauty of the little piece of earth she'd been given to tend. Today, right now, she would focus on that.

Judge Yancy popped into her mind and she remembered that she'd promised to go see him. Glancing at her watch, she saw that it was nearly one and she had to be at the wolf center to sign for the fencing when it arrived. She'd have to put off her visit to him.

Pausing on the dirt road—no one else would likely be on it, anyway—she called up the call history on her cell phone and found the judge's number. "Yancy, here," he said. The years of southern living lazed around his soft consonants.

"Hi, Judge. It's Desi Rousseau. How's Lacey?"

"'Bout the same, I reckon."

"All right. How about if I come by and see her later this afternoon? I've got to meet the fencing people and get my assistant going on the patch job. Maybe around four-thirty?"

"Well, I was hoping to serve you some lunch." He sounded slightly annoyed.

Desi frowned. The last thing in the world she wanted was another irritation. "Look," she said with an edge to her voice, "it's been a bad morning. I appreciate your support and I'm not trying to blow you off, I'm just *swamped,* all right?"

A pause, thick with reaction, stretched between them, and Desi's heart sank. The last thing in the world she needed was to lose one of her very few allies.

But when he spoke, he said only, "You're right, honey. Sorry about that. You need any help?"

"No, but thanks for the offer." She tried to smile, but a sense of foreboding thickened in her lungs. "I'll see you after a while."

* * *

It was one damned thing after another, Tam thought as his cell phone rang in his pocket when he was—finally—leaving the pub, the box of freezer-burned meats under his arm. He glanced at the screen and recognized the number as belonging to his dead mate Roger's wife. For a minute he hesitated, thumb hovering over the button. She'd been devastated by Roger's death and he wanted to be there for her, but today his mind was on other things.

Oh, don't be an arse, he thought, and punched the button. "Hello, Zara. How are you today?"

"Hi, Tam. Are you busy?"

He'd had some practice with the levels of despair in her voice. Today she sounded fairly good. "Not so much, eh. I'm about to hop in my car and take some meat to a wolf sanctuary. What's up?"

"It's nothing very much today, honestly. I was wondering if you could come to town and help me settle some things with Roger's estate sometime soon."

The drive was nearly 150 miles, one way, to Denver. Driving these days caused a lot of pain in the leg he'd shattered in the same accident that killed Roger. "How'd you like to drive up to Mariposa, instead, sweet? It's gorgeous up here, and there's plenty of room for you."

"Really?"

"Sure, why not?" He shifted the box on his arm, putting it on the roof of the car. "I'll have to work a bit, but we can maybe get out and have a tramp through the woods. How'd you like that?"

Her voice sweetened. "That would be really great, Tam. I'd love it. I'll see what's going on with work and give you a call at the start of next week. How's that?"

"Good. Anything else?"

"No, thanks. Except—how are things with you?"

He glanced up to the tops of the craggy peaks, to the sunlight cascading down the mountain sides and dancing on the clear, thin ice covering the stream. A memory of Desi Rousseau's unbound breasts, moving gently beneath her sweater this morning crossed his internal vision. "Can't complain," he said, and managed to keep the impatience out of his voice.

"I'm glad."

"Well, give me a call next week, eh? We'll figure it out then."

They hung up, and Tam was happy to get moving. The day was bitter beneath the warmth, so he zipped his thick coat up to the neck and slapped on a stocking cap. There was snow in the wind.

By the time he made it up the mountain to Desi's place, long shadows were falling across the high meadows and the sun was nothing more than a ribbon of soft gold along the edges of the peaks. He spied Desi, wearing a pair of overalls that hid her voluptuous curves, wrestling with a length of wire fencing.

"Hello!" he cried as he got out of the car. "Need some help?"

She shook her hair out of her face. "I'd love it. It needs to get finished by dark and I'm pushing it." As he approached, she pointed. "If you'd keep that part stretched tight, I can get it fastened."

He did as he was told, and wordlessly squatted to stretch the lower piece when she'd done the top. She was quick and skillful, her gloved hands working with clean efficiency, her attention fixed wholly on her task.

"One more," she said, straightening. "Then we're done."

He walked to the next post, and it was plain that a wide section had simply been cut out of the fence. Tam touched the severed ends. "No idea who did it, eh?"

Gripping her wire cutters, she stretched the fence and slid a thumb through one square. "I have my theories," she said. "Hold that, would you?"

He grabbed it. "Theories?"

"Developers want the land. Several developers. It's worth a fortune with the hot springs and the meadow, which is buildable."

He glanced over his shoulder at the kennels, encircled by a stand of long-needled pines with cinnamon-colored trunks. It was grassy and wide and currently filled with a handful of wolves, watching them curiously. Wind ruffled the fur of a big, dark gray one. His dark yellow eyes seemed lit from behind as they bored into Tam. Primeval hackles rose on his spine. "He's a scary one."

Desi raised her head. "He's a rescue from Montana. They'd kept him in a garage for three years. He's not, understandably, all that friendly to humans."

"Are you afraid of them?"

Securing the last section of fence, she stood up and looked back to them. "I'm respectful. I know they could kill me. But I've also been careful to establish my authority. Wolves are hierarchal, and they respect the pecking order very seriously. Juneau is the alpha, but he lets me share leadership."

"Would they let me touch them?"

"Some will. Not him." She looked up at him, smiled slightly. "He senses that you're an alpha. Give him some time and he might."

"Am I?"

She rolled her eyes, straightened. "You try to pretend you're just a charming second, but wolves know."

"And so do you."

She nodded. "If you want, you can help me gather my tools."

"All right."

To his disappointment, her extraordinary fall of hair was bound up in a heavy braid. He supposed such hair was impractical when she was working, but he found his eyes on the end of it, and he thought about pulling the bright pink rubber band off and unweaving that richness of hair.

He hurried to catch up with her, conscious of the sore muscles above his knees from snowshoeing yesterday. "Any sign of the wolf?"

"Not yet."

"She'll turn up, yeah?"

She lifted a shoulder, let it fall. "I don't know." She turned to let him catch up. "And somebody shot the other wolf for some unknown reason, so Fir isn't safe out there at all."

A soft, pale twilight sank into the clearing, and cold blew out from beneath the trees. A mist, thick and somehow out of place, rose just beyond the trees. He caught a scent that made him think, fiercely and suddenly, of home—his youthful home, when his mother was still alive, before he'd gone to live with his grandparents. "What's there?" he asked, pointing.

"The hot springs," she said, and dropped her gloves and wire cutters into a red tool box. "Would you like to see them?"

"I really would." He glanced at the car. "Don't let me forget I brought you some meat for the wolves, and the donations from the jar. Forty-three dollars."

Her smile, showing that deep dimple, was reward enough. In addition, she leaned forward and kissed his cheek, squeezing his hands. "Tam! Thank you!"

She smelled like lemons. A suspiciously hot sensation burned his ears. Was he *flustered?* Surely not.

"Not a problem," he said. Patted her upper arm, which was surprisingly solid.

"The spring is this way," she said, and waved him toward a path tamped down in the snow beneath the trees. It was darker there, mysterious, full of sounds that could be animals—or spirits. He paused, listening, raising his head toward the heather sky he could glimpse through the arrows of trees.

"This is a holy place, yeah?"

Desi paused and turned to look up at him with a sharp, measuring expression on her face. "Some think so."

He stood there, listening, and it was possible to almost make out the whispers, the spirits speaking among themselves. "I fancy I can hear the trees speaking," he said, with a wry little smile so she wouldn't think him daft. "Like a forest in a fairy tale."

The dark surface of her eyes showed a rippling, like wind over water. "Right over there," she said, pointing into the trees, "was a graveyard. The bodies were not buried, but put on platforms. It's very sacred ground, and one of the things I'd like to keep holy."

Tam touched his chest. "Didn't the Indians have something to say about you getting the land?"

"It belonged to a ranch, all this land did. It was huge, like 500,000 acres or something like that. When it was first settled, the Indians here didn't have much say over anything." She paused, then seemed to decide something. Turning in the direction she had pointed, she ducked under the trees and waved for him to follow. They tramped through the snow, sometimes quite deep, for a few hundred feet, then paused. A small Indian symbol, clouds and lightning, topped a hand-lettered sign covered in a laminate. The sign said: "Please do not cross this sacred line of trees. It is the council ground of our ancestors and we wish to respect their peace. Mariposa Ute Council."

"I gave them the land back," Desi said.

"How did you know what it was?"

She pointed to a treehouse sort of structure. A spine of a feather, attached by a cord, blew in the wind. He blinked, and it disappeared. "I could tell what it was, but to be sure, I asked Helene about it. Do you know Josh's mother?"

"I've met her once or twice."

"She's a medicine woman, a very honored teacher."

A whistle, high and eerie, wound through the trees. Tam felt his body tense. "What was that?"

The dimple flashed in her white cheek. "Are you scared?"

He shrugged, trying to get the ghosties off his neck. "Not exactly. But I wouldn't mind moving on."

Desi laughed, but she tugged his sleeve to bring him back to the path. Steam billowed up in clouds as they came toward a clearing, and he eagerly pushed forward. "I grew up in Rotorua," he said. "Till I was twelve, anyway. It's like Yellowstone here—geysers and boiling mud and all that. I miss the geology of it."

"Well, this is less dramatic, but very healing."

The snowy path emptied into a bowl of land dominated by a wide pool, shining a soft lavender color in the gloaming. A waterfall poured down a grotto. Steam rose in clouds from it. "Must be pretty hot, yeah?"

Desi gestured. "Be my guest. Feel it."

The air smelled of minerals and earth. Gladly he moved forward, thinking how good that water would be for his bum leg. He stuck his hand in the pool and let go of a long sigh. "Brilliant," he said, and stood back up. In the shadows of the trees to the north, he saw a low hut, shaped like a beehive.

She saw the direction of his gaze. "Helene is my teacher, too," she said, but didn't elaborate. "It's a sweat lodge."

He didn't push. Settling on a rock by the pool, he inhaled the scent of steam and mountain and impending night, the hint of sulfur that seemed to always accompany hot springs. He pointed to another rock opposite. "Take a load off, will you?"

She hesitated, sticking her hands in her pockets. "I've got a lot to do before I stop today."

"I'll help you. Sit for a minute." When she still did not move, he added, "You look knackered, love. We won't stay long."

Desi nodded and came forward, gingerly perching on the rock opposite him as if he were Bacchus himself, ready to blow in his pipes and call an orgy.

"I miss that smell," he said. "When I was a lad, that was what I smelled morning noon and night."

"I think you really miss it, don't you?"

"Sometimes."

"So why stay here?"

Tam rubbed a hollow place in his chest. "Me mum died when I was twelve and I was sent up north to live with her parents. They died, too." He smiled to show it was long ago. "There's nothing there for me now."

For a minute Desi looked at him. Then she nodded and slapped her legs. "Well, I know a baby wolf who needs feeding. Would you like to do that?"

"Yes," he said. "I'd like it a lot."

Chapter 5

As they walked back toward the caretaker's cabin, Desi scolded herself internally with a litany of cautions that came down to one:

Don't fall under his spell.

And if he'd been only charming or good-looking, she might have found it easier to resist, but there was something good and honest about him, something that felt steady and real. Sturdy. Unmoving.

At his car she waited while he fetched the box he'd brought from the pub, then gestured for him to follow as she headed up the hill on a path tramped out in the snow. At the caretaker's cabin, a lamp showed through the high line of windows just beneath the eaves.

Inside she stomped snow off her boots. "You want some tea?"

Tam stayed by the door. "Want me to take off my shoes?"

"Not necessary." She came close enough to take the box from him, and peeked inside. Despite herself, she gasped. She'd been expecting a little of this and that, scraps. This was a heavy box full of all kinds of meat. "Oh, this is excellent, Tam!"

"No problem. And, yeah, I'd love tea."

She pointed to the small kitchenette area, a stove the size of a butane tank, a fridge like a television. "If you wouldn't mind, then, put the kettle on and I'll run this meat out to the feed house and bring the pup back."

"Am I making you nervous, Desi?"

"No!" she lied breathlessly. "Why would you say so?"

Tam looked at her mouth openly, rubbing his chest. She didn't move immediately. "Just a feeling," he said quietly.

Her eyes were on his mouth. A sensual mouth, with an almost overly full lower lip. Beneath it, the smallest possible fringe of hair, squarely below the middle of his lip. A strong, square chin.

The air around them thickened, seemed edged with a smoky resonance. Desi felt something walk down her spine as she raised her eyes to his, to the pale green that was so startling and beautiful, a curious softness in the powerfully male arrangement of features.

He swallowed. "Go on now, get the pup," he said. "I'll put on the tea."

Desi shook herself out of the little dream. Stung

and flustered, she took a step backward and glared up at him. "I told you to stop that!"

He let go of a chuckle of surprise. "Stop what?"

"Trying to charm me. Turning on all the little quirks and tricks."

He raised a brow. "Like that, you mean?"

"It's just impossible for you not to do it, isn't it?" She rolled her eyes, hiked the box closer to her chest. "Attempt to charm every woman you come into contact with?"

His eyes narrowed. "I don't think I deserved that one, mate. Did it cross your mind that it might not be *all* women, but you in particular?"

She rolled her eyes. "Right."

His body went still, and Desi regretted her meanness. But he said mildly, "Not every man is a bastard like that husband of yours."

Desi lowered her head. "Did you know him?"

Tam just nodded.

"I guess everyone did." It was difficult to keep the bitterness from her tone. "There's not a soul in Mariposa who doesn't know he was cheating on me for heaven knows how long." She pushed hair out of her eyes, blinking hard. "I shouldn't be surprised."

"The surprise is how he landed a woman like you."

She looked at him. A thousand replies and versions of replies arrived in her mind, but in the end none of them seemed right.

"I know you've had a bad time," Tam said. "But don't start thinking all men are bastards. We're not, you know."

She nodded. "I'll be back in a minute."

"Two shakes of a dead lamb's tail," he quipped.

She wanted to chuckle at his joke. Instead, she rushed out, box in her arms, to avoid showing even a hint of emotion.

When Desi returned with the pup, she'd managed to calm down a little. There was something about Tamati Neville that was stirring her up in ways she had not known in a long time. *Beware,* said a little voice.

It's too soon, said her sister's voice.

The sleepy pup yawned beneath her throat, and Desi buried her face close as she ducked back into the cabin. "You're such a little sweetheart," she said. His fur, still baby soft, smelled of the straw they used for the pens, and that earthy, furry undernote of wolf and the pervasiveness of baby. Milk, she thought, and bent close to his mouth. Happily he licked her nose. Desi laughed.

As she came into the cabin, Tam was pouring hot water into a round yellow pot and he'd set out mugs and spoons and sugar. "You take milk?" he asked.

"Yes. But I'll finish that. You come sit down and take the baby."

Tam moved to the couch and sat down, that limp barely noticeable today. Desi put the baby into his lap and tried to avoid looking into those astonishing eyes. God, what was wrong with her? She didn't get like this, all flushed and flustered by a man.

But as he reached for the pup, his fingers grazed her left breast, and she was quite sure it was not on purpose. Their eyes met for a split second, silent acknowledgment, then slid away. "Hey, baby," Tam said to the pup. "Good to see you again."

The pup whimpered in happiness and took the bottle. Desi headed toward the kitchen area and finished making the tea. Darkness was falling beyond the windows and her stomach growled. Tam chuckled. "You should have brought some more lamb stew home for your supper."

Desi brought everything over on a tray. "That was excellent food." She stirred sugar into her tea. "But it was also a long time ago."

"It was." He scratched the wolf's forehead. "If you've got a bikkie or something like that, I wouldn't mind it."

"Bikkie?"

"Biscuit?" He paused. "Cookies."

"Ah." Desi's stomach growled again, and she stood up to look in the cupboards. There wasn't much there, but she found some graham crackers and brought them over.

"I had a visitor this morning you might want to know about," Tam said.

"I'm listening."

"Me old girlfriend. She's just married Bill Biloxi. They've got the land next to yours."

The dog door flew open and a dog, then another came through like rockets, first Tecumseh, then Sitting Bull. "Hey, guys!" she cried. "Where have you been?"

The dogs, fluffy and covered with snow, shook themselves hard, looking back to the dog door. Desi gave Tam a grin and held up a hand, ticking off seconds on her fingers. "One, two, three, four, five—" the door flew upward and the third wolf-mix came through, nails skittering on the floor.

"Ah, there you are!" she said to Crazy Horse, always the laggard of the group and the sweetest. He rushed over, his entire rear half wiggling, and licked her hand, then greeted Tam, as well. "Hey, honey, whatcha been up to?"

"Are these wolves?" Tam asked.

"Tecumseh more so than the other two," she said, pointing to her big, fluffy wolf-mix. "But these are my dogs. They're all pretty domesticated. I've had Sitting Bull for a long time, and Crazy Horse is a pretty recent rescue. He was abandoned, and he's the sweetest thing you ever saw." She lifted his big nose and kissed the velvety top of it. His eyes drifted closed and he made a soft, growling noise of pleasure. "And a big baby, too, huh?"

Tam laughed, the sound warm and low. Desi realized she'd let her guard down again.

But she was tired. It had been a long day. There was time to reestablish distance tomorrow. For now he was easy to be around, and it was easy to just be…herself.

"You were saying about your old girlfriend?" she prompted.

"Right. They want to open a spa and utilize the hot springs."

"I'd heard that."

"You realize that you could lose the flow to your land if they succeed?"

She raised her eyebrows, hand lingering in the pile of Crazy Horse's fur. "I hadn't thought of that." It made her feel guilty, not realizing that, but she'd just been overwhelmed with the mess with Claude.

He lifted an eyebrow. "Thing is, you can probably get an injunction to stop them."

"On what grounds?"

"The flow of hot springs is compromised when anyone taps into it more than they should. Interferes with the disbursement of heat and water."

Desi looked at him for a minute, then smiled. "That's very smart, Tam."

He winked. "I aim to please."

"Or get back at her."

"Nah. My motives are to help you."

Desi nibbled a graham cracker. "In theory, it's a great idea, but I suspect I might have trouble getting anyone to rally around my cause." Her heart felt hollow as she considered the reality. "Everyone thinks I killed Claude." With a frown she said, "It took me so long to win a place in Mariposa, and I was the one who did all the work, all the community building, and he reaped the benefits."

"It's a hard community to crack," he said.

"Yeah, it really isn't fair that not only did he cheat on me publicly, but he managed to get himself murdered, which ruined my reputation and made me lose all my connections in the community." She broke a cracker, stared at it with a tight mouth. "I never had a place to call mine. Mariposa was."

"It will be again," Tam said. "Eventually the murderer will be found and you'll be steady and here and they'll think you're a heroine."

Desi smiled ruefully. "It's a nice picture. Thanks."

"In the meantime, I bet you can get the Utes on your side with that injunction, eh?"

"You know," she said, "you might just have something there."

"Good," he said, and settled the sleeping wolf cub beside him on the couch. The baby, absolutely trusting, stretched his feet out in front of him and sighed hard.

"You injured your leg in the Hayman fire?"

He rubbed the thigh vigorously for a minute. "I did."

"What happened?"

"Bad landing," he said. "We misjudged it. I had a spiral fracture of the bones in my thigh and shattered my knee. Roger tried to help, but he was trapped by a falling tree." His face showed nothing, which gave Desi an even deeper sympathy for his loss.

"I'm sorry," she said.

"Life brings what she brings, yeah?"

The pup stretched and made a soft yawning noise. "So much for teaching him to be wild eventually," Desi said

A guilty expression crossed Tam's face. "Sorry. Did I—"

"No. I probably knew as soon as he arrived that it wasn't going to happen. Especially not without a wolf mother to teach him." The thought of Fir sent pangs of loss through her middle. "But we should be careful about letting him bond too much to you."

"Understood," he said. "He needs his adoptive mum and his pack, yeah?"

Desi nodded. "Yes. Wish I knew where she is."

"I have time in the morning, I could come out and help track her."

"Do you know how to do that?"

"I do, love." He stuck out his chest in a mocking pose. "I was trained to do many things in my smoke jumping days."

She nodded. "Please. Any help you can offer would be wonderful."

"I will, then." He stood. "Now, I suppose I'd best let you get your work done, eh? Can I help you with anything else before I go?"

Desi shook her head. "You've been a great help already today, Tam. Thank you." She stood up with him, a warmth in her chest. "It's nice to make a new friend."

He took her hand, a faint irony in the tilt of his head. "I have more than friendship on *my* mind, love."

Desi tried to take her hand away, but he just grinned and held on, not tugging or pushing, just holding on. "I'm not—this isn't…ugh!" She scowled up at him.

His grin broadened. "Do you like me?"

"Yeah. You're a nice guy."

"Only nice?" He tugged her hand a little bit, and Desi had no choice but to move forward. "You're not finding anything exciting?"

She looked up at him, shaking her head. "Tam, I—"

With one quick move he neatly folded her arm behind her, his arm around her waist, their bodies in full contact. A hot jolt of desire moved through her, and she tried to find a protest, but his mouth captured hers, gobbling up her words.

Desi heard a faint noise rise in her throat at the shock of his lips upon her own, the nudge of his tongue shifting her mouth open. His body was as solid and steady as it appeared. Her breasts were crushed into his chest, her hips hard against his, her thighs—oh!—laced.

And Tam very slowly, very pointedly, very thoroughly kissed her. It was greeting and promise and exploration, his tongue asking hers to dance, then leading the kiss into a waltz of grace and beauty, the exact pause, the soft nibble on her lower lip, the softness of his breath on her cheek. His free hand rose and covered her cheek, his fingers grazing the edge of her eye, her ear. Such a big hand. Such a skilled kiss. Against her pubic bone, she felt the rise of his member, a warm unfurling. An answering heat blossomed in her breasts, and she found herself rubbing, almost unconsciously, against his chest.

He made a low, rich noise and pulled her more closely against him, his tongue going deeper, drawing hers back into the hot depths of his mouth.

Danger, danger, danger!

She opened her eyes and saw that his eyes were closed, the black lashes fanning over his dark cheeks. As if he sensed her gaze, he opened his eyes, and their gazes locked. Holding her gaze, Tam suckled lightly on her lower lip, and heat slammed into her hips, softening her belly, her knees, as if she were his doll, opening at his will.

She pushed at him, backing away with her hand to her lips. "I can't do this. It's too much. It's too…I don't have good judgment right now."

He caught her hand, and before she could run away entirely, lifted it to his lips. "You don't have to be anyone or do anything."

Letting her go, he shrugged into his coat and turned up the collar. "I'll see you soon, Desdemona."

And then he was gone.

As she walked down the hill to her own cabin, Desi felt the kiss rocketing over her flesh, swirling over her nape, slamming into the back of her knees and the crook of her elbow. He tasted of promise—the long, lazy promise of sex that lasted hours and hours, unrushed and easy and building to—

No.

Breathing the sharpness of winter darkness, she cooled her overheated throat and belly and imagination. Her life was an absolute mess, and so were her emotions. The last thing she needed was to get mixed up with some hot-blooded sweet-talker who'd just break her heart all over again.

By the time she returned to her house, Desi was starving half to death, but it was too late to prepare the chili she'd planned, and she settled for a grilled cheese sandwich and a handful of pretzel sticks with a cup of instant coffee.

Her sisters both howled over her love of instant coffee, but she'd grown fond of it during college, when she borrowed her roommate's electric kettle and learned to drink crystallized coffee with powdered cream. On her travels she carried instant coffee, and when she and Claude had purchased the land, they'd had little in the way of comforts for a long time, so instant coffee and hot chocolate were a couple of their favorite things.

In a way, she thought, her reliance on instant coffee was a symbol of her life. Carrying the cup to the fire, she settled in an easy chair in front of the round, hot stove. Cozy, she thought, extending her toes in their woolen socks toward the warmth. The dogs were scattered in piles around the room, Sitting Bull snoring through his big snout, Tecumseh running in his sleep, paws flipping in his hurry.

The phone rang and Desi sighed. It was across the room on the counter. If she could be sure it was a personal call, she'd leave it, but with a veterinary business, she had to answer. Reluctantly, praying it wasn't some terrible emergency like a shot goat or a mauled horse, she stood up and grabbed it. "Dr. Rousseau."

"Hey, girl, did you forget your old judge?"

Horrified, Desi covered her mouth. "I am so sorry! I've been working on the hole in the fence all day and just got finished. How is Lacey?"

"Fine, fine," he said gruffly. "She'll be all right, but I'm disappointed, Desdemona. I fixed your favorite butternut squash soup."

"I'm so sorry," Desi repeated. "I guess I've been overwhelmed. Can I sample the soup tomorrow?"

"I'll save you some," he said. "What time can I expect you?"

"Ten o'clock?"

"Right. I'll see you then, sweetheart."

"Bye, Judge. Thanks for your understanding." She flipped the phone closed and thought about the things that needed to be done tomorrow. She needed to spend some time at the clinic in the afternoon, and see the judge in the morning and catch Helene at some point, too. She scrolled through her address book on the phone, and found Helene's number. She punched the call button and waited for Helene's voice mail.

Instead, the real woman answered. "Hello, Desi!" she cried.

"Hi, Helene. I'm surprised to get you—don't you usually work Thursday nights?"

"A girl needed to pick up some hours, so I let her have them. How are you holding up, girl? Your sister told me somebody cut your fence."

"Yeah. Listen, I have something to talk to you about—do you have some time in the morning, before ten, say?"

"You know me. Up at the crack of dawn. You want to come have breakfast with me and Glory? I'll make pancakes."

"That sounds great. I'll be there at what? Eight?"

"Perfect."

The morning meetings arranged, Desi headed back to the fireside chair and the dogs. A gust of wind slammed into the house, and she whirled as a window flew open, letting the wind roll into the room in a ball that scared the dogs into full alert. They jumped up, Sitting Bull barking fiercely, his hackles raised.

Desi took her rifle off the wall, checked it and peered out into the night. Nothing but wind as far as she could tell, but in the distance the wolves howled.

Damn. What if there was someone out there again? Hassling the wolves? She picked up the cell phone and dialed Alex, the caretaker. He answered immediately. "I'm on it, boss. Don't worry."

"Be careful," she said.

"You know it."

Slamming her feet into her boots and donning heavy winter gear, she gripped the rifle and went outside to check the perimeter of her own clearing. The dogs moved with her as a group, Tecumseh in the lead, Sitting Bull and Crazy Horse flanking her protectively.

The night was very dark with no moon and no clouds to reflect the town lights back down to the forest. Once away from the island of light that was her cabin, Desi could see little at all. The trees formed a black wall around the meadow, and there were no prints she could see in the snow. She turned in a careful circle, listening.

Nothing. The dogs looked and panted, sniffed the snow, but when they gave up and sat down, Desi knew she was all right. Against her thigh, her cell phone rang. "Nothing here," Alex said.

"Here, either. Maybe it was the ghosts," she said.

"Musta been."

"See you in the morning. Call me if you hear anything else." She headed back to the house, locked up and hung her coat on the hook.

Next to Claude's woven serape. It hung where he'd left it, one of the few things she hadn't boxed up and given away. It seemed to mock her now. She reached for it, hesitated, then annoyed with her weakness, she grabbed it from the hook, planning to carry it into the back room.

But from the depths of the fabric came a scent. Fur and snow and dogs, woodsmoke and vanilla cookies and shampoo. Almost without realizing what she was doing, Desi carried the fabric to her nose and inhaled it, flooded by a hundred memories, a thousand. Claude laughing as a hoard of little kids mobbed him in the streets in Peru, after the peppermints they knew he carried in his pockets. Claude standing at the top of a mountain overlooking a vast, empty landscape, his hair flying loose on a wind. Claude kissing her. Telling her she was beautiful, the most beautiful woman in the world.

Claude painting. Proudly showing her the first of his canvases, and her slight shame in realizing that she hadn't expected him to be particularly good. And he was. Not, perhaps, a genius, but clear-eyed, with a distinctive style.

Realizing what she was doing, Desi dropped the serape in horror. It lay in a puddle at her feet, and she stared at it as if it was a snake, waiting to coil around her ankles and squeeze her to death. How could she be thinking of those things? He'd been terrible to her! He'd lied and cheated—not only to Desi, but to at least three other women she knew of. Played them all like the Pied Piper, and they'd all danced to his flute like little puppets.

And yet…was anyone all bad?

Tears welled in her eyes. The third time in as many days, and she *never* cried. Furious with herself and the flood of emotions she didn't understand, she roared, kicking the serape across the room. It puddled by the table harmlessly, but Desi stomped into the small room where Claude had once worked and flung open the closet where she had stowed his paintings. There were dozens of them, small and large. And sketches and abandoned pieces. She hauled them out, thinking she'd take them down the mountain in the morning and fling them on the dentist's wife's lawn.

In the battered bureau were his paints and brushes and tablets of paper, his charcoals and photos he'd taken to use as models. She flung it all into boxes, refusing to halt to look at any of it.

She could burn it all. The paintings and sketches and supplies. Make a bonfire out of his foolishness, his arrogance, the shallowness that had, in the end, gotten him killed.

"You idiot!" she cried, throwing a small portrait of the dogs into the box.

Then she rescued it. The dogs were hers, too. She wanted this one.

In the other room her cell phone rang, and Desi looked up, surprised. She never had so many calls in a single evening. It rang again and she rushed to answer it. "Dr. Rousseau," she said.

"Hey, Doc, how are ya?"

In surprise, Desi asked, "Miranda? Is that you, sis?"

"It is. How's life in Yawnsville?"

"As thrilling as ever." Desi looked over her shoulder at the bonfire materials. "To what do I owe the honor of this call?" Miranda lived in Manhattan, an artist herself. She rarely kept in contact with the family, and in fact, Desi thought she was in Europe. "When did you get back?"

"Couple of days ago. I've been kind of worried about you. There's a lot of talk about Claude's work in art circles."

"There is? Why?"

"Murder. Scandal. Good-looking man. Makes a good story."

"You know," she said, glancing over her shoulder at the stuff in the back room, "I was just thinking I might make a bonfire out of all the stuff he left here. It might be a way to rid myself of his—" She almost said *spirit*. But she didn't believe in things like that, in ghosts and all that nonsense. "—presence," she substituted.

"Burn his clothes if you like, but I wouldn't burn the paintings if I were you." She paused, and her smoky, beautifully resonant voice took on a layer of irony. "They're going to be worth a lot of money."

"Why do you say that?"

"I'm calling to warn you that there's a cable show on tonight about him. An art dealer is behind it—

Renate Franz—a German with a Manhattan gallery who wants to get the frenzy going."

Something about the name rang a bell, but Desi didn't immediately place it. "I'm not following you, Miranda. Speak slowly in words of one syllable. I've had a hell of a day."

"I'd put money on some news crew picking this up. Lay low."

"Oh, great." That was all she needed. "Thanks for the warning."

"You don't sound great tonight, sissy."

"Only you can get away with calling me that, you know," Desi said, grinning.

Miranda gave a low chuckle. "I know."

"I'm fine," Desi said. "If you want to come visit, save it for the springtime. Juliet is going to marry Josh in May."

"She called me. I'm very happy for her, but that would mean dealing with parents, and you know I don't do that."

"You can't skip Juliet's wedding, Miranda."

"I don't want to. But—"

Desi took on her most forbidding elder-sister tone. "Juliet would be devastated if you didn't come. You *will* be here. I'll run interference with our parents."

"You're right. I need to come." She sounded tired. "It would be good to get a break, too. I've been working really hard."

"Good. You're welcome anytime, kiddo," she said. "Anytime."

"Thanks, Desi. Insure the paintings, huh?"

"Will do."

As she hung up, Desi shook her head. She was never going to escape Claude Tsosie. The thought left a weight on her shoulders so heavy she felt as stooped as an old woman.

Somehow she had to get him out of her head, her thoughts, her house.

Her life.

Chapter 6

At dawn Tam tied his heavy boots, flung his snow-shoes over his shoulder and jumped in his car to head up to Orchid Pass. The reason for its name was obvious as he pulled off the road at the trailhead—lines of craggy, high peaks, all well above timberline and frosted heavily with snow, glowed a soft pinkish purple with dawn. The sky above was a thick purpled blue, as if it could be sliced.

Tam strapped on his snowshoes, tugged on his gloves and hat and set off on the trail. He knew it well, but in his backpack was a compass and map, along with waterproof matches and packets of concentrated nourishment and emergency blankets. Only a fool went into the mountains unprepared.

He'd been dreaming of the she-wolf this morning, and in his imagination, she'd been lost and huddled by a small lake he knew of up here. It hurt nothing to see if there was any weight to the vision. And anyway, he liked to get out and do something vigorous every day.

There was nothing so pristine as the mountains in the morning, winter or summer. The thin air let through a brilliance of sunlight, and there was no scent of humankind, only trees and snow or earth and water. No sound of engines. No music. Utter stillness reigned, just the sound of his own breath, moistening the wool scarf over his nose and mouth, and the squeak of the snowshoes on the vast blanket of snow, the small plops of snow falling from branches.

Against the depth of serenity the place gave him, he felt the press of his sudden and surprising wish for Desi Rousseau. Her body, her hair, her mouth. Although the suspicion in her eyes last night had taken him unaware.

A Buddhist retreat had occupied the farm next to his grandfather's place near Cape Reinga, and he'd become friends with some of the…what were they called? Priests? They believed that yearning, desire, was the source of all unhappiness, and while Tam had never particularly believed it, this morning he could see that his desire for the prickly veterinarian was like sandpaper against his peacefulness, a jolt of jagged red through his orchid morning.

Not so easy was Desdemona. She was a porcupine and a cat and a blue jay, all rolled into one intriguing

and difficult package. He could not understand why
he felt so protective of her.

But he did. He felt protective and curious. And
more. He wanted to take down her hair and peel away
her layers and layers of clothes to see the body beneath. He wanted to see her let go of that calm and
fierceness and explode in an orgasm that would carry
her into the next part of her life.

Most of all he wanted to wipe away the memory
of the smirking face of Claude Tsosie, wanted her to
see that a man could desire her for herself.

In the stillness of the pink-washed dawn, he
snowshoed through the trees, looking for tracks and
signs. He saw the thin, clustered tracks of deer, the
triangular scratches of bird feet, even the obvious
roughness where a larger animal had rolled and
rubbed its back on the trunk of a tree. Bear? No, he
thought they hibernated. Mountain lion? He shuddered. He didn't fancy meeting claws and teeth of
that size.

The lake was a couple of miles in, and he was feeling agreeably exercised by the time he arrived. It
wasn't possible to really see the lake. It was buried
beneath three or four feet of snow and iced over beneath that, but the oval of it lay in the clearing in patient expectation of spring.

Tam suddenly felt foolish. He'd dreamed of the
wolf because he wanted to see the pup have a mum.
Or maybe he wanted to be a hero in Desi's eyes. But
to follow the prompting of a dream was silly.

Still, he was here, wasn't he? Methodically he

crisscrossed the open expanse, looking for signs of the wolf, sure he would not find them.

So, when he caught sight of a scarlet spill of blood on the white snow beneath a tree, his heart caught. He snowshoed over, his knee aching a bit, and to his amazement, saw the obvious signs of a hunt-and-kill. A jackrabbit, or squirrel, maybe even a large bird. He saw no evidence of carcass or feathers.

There *were* the unmistakable prints of a dog. A wolf. Trotting away from the kill site. A ripple of surprise and excitement rushed down his spine. What were the chances?

Except they said animals communicated, telepathically, in pictures, which was why a person would suddenly get an urge to go to the door and see if the cat wanted in and find the cat sitting there waiting.

The tracks headed into the trees, and he marked the sun to find his direction. The wolf was headed southeast, back toward home, if Tam had his mental map right. As the crow flew, the sanctuary was only three or four miles.

Too much of a hike overland for Tam's tired knee, however. He headed back to his truck. He'd drive to Desi's place and tell her what he'd seen. He tried not to notice how the thought cheered him.

Desi had just made a pot of tea when the dogs started barking in a frenzy. Scowling, she peered out the window, praying it wasn't the sheriff again. After the long day yesterday, she was sore and tired—and the last thing in the world she wanted was more harassment. She had to see the judge this morning, and she needed to talk to Helene about a possible injunction, spend some time looking for the missing wolf and maybe, just maybe, do something relaxing or fun this afternoon. Maybe go see her sister and talk wedding details.

She didn't recognize the tall brunette woman who climbed out of a fully loaded SUV with the telltale pristineness of a rental. The woman was strikingly beautiful. She wore jeans on her long legs, and a high-end, powder-blue parka and a perky knitted hat of the same color. Sometimes, visitors to the area made a wrong turn on their way to various ski slopes, and Desi suspected that was the case here. She grabbed her own, far more battered parka and stepped out on the porch. "Hi, can I help you?"

The woman smiled, showing a toothy, very white smile and eyes the color of Delft china. "Are you Desdemona?"

She suddenly had a bad feeling about this. "Who's asking?" she crossed her arms and tried to look grouchy.

"I'm Abby Danmark, from KZZZ-TV in Denver." She gestured to someone behind her, and a man came around with a camera on his shoulder. Desi started backing away, shaking her head. "I'd like to interview you."

Maybe she could shame them. "About the wolves?" she asked and smiled. The dogs were sitting on the porch with her, watching. The reporter gave them a nervous eye. "It would be better to go up to the sanctuary for that." She brushed hair off her face. "And I'm hardly television ready. Do you want to make an appointment for later this afternoon?"

"We want to talk about Claude, Desdemona."

"You may call me Dr. Rousseau," Desi said stiffly. "But I will not talk about Claude for television." She stood firm. "You can get off my land now."

"But Dr. Rousseau, wouldn't you like a chance to tell your side?"

"You ambush me and want me to be nice to you?" Desi smiled bitterly. "Please, just go." Whistling to the dogs, she turned to go inside.

"Desdemona, they're talking about you all over the art world. It's quite a triangle. You and Christie Lundgren and the paintings."

Another engine rumbled up the road, and the woman turned to see who was coming. Desi shook her head and ducked into the house, slamming the door. She fell backward against it and let go of a roar of frustration. "Enough already!" she cried to the heavens and anyone who might be listening. "I'm tired! Make it stop!"

The sound of the second vehicle pulling into the circular drive sent the dogs into alert again, and she gave them a command to stay as she went to the window over the kitchen sink to look out, fearing it would be another reporter or the sheriff or more trouble.

Instead, the sturdy, solid personage of Tamati Neville stepped out of the truck and slammed the door behind him with calm but somehow threatening strength. She heard him say, "Can I help you?"

The cameras were no doubt rolling. Desi didn't care. She was so relieved to see a friendly face that she stepped out on the porch again. "Hi, Tam. Breakfast is just about ready. Come eat."

The reporter signaled the cameraman to film and she kept after Tam, asking questions as he solidly plainly ignored her. When his back was to them, he gave her a questioning glance. She just shook her head. "Come inside," she said. As he passed her, she said to the reporter, "Now take your cameras and leave my land or I'll call the sheriff."

"Dr. Rousseau, if you change your mind, just call my station. You have a right to tell your side of the story, too."

That gave Desi pause. "Then why didn't you just call me and ask for it?"

The woman lifted a shoulder, and her full, beautiful lips curled into a rueful smile, making Desi think of the actress Geena Davis. "I like to ski."

Shaking her head, Desi went inside and closed the door firmly. Tam waited for her, looking athletic and hale in a ski jacket and close-fitting ski pants that showed his astoundingly shapely legs and butt. "God, I'm glad to see you!" she said with a sigh, and then couldn't help stating the obvious. "And my, my, my," she said, putting her hands on her hips. "Do you ever look great in a pair of ski pants."

He grinned rakishly and turned in a circle slowly. "Happy to oblige."

For one instant Desi forgot everything in her life. All the annoyances and pressures, all the grim predictions for her future, even the wolves, and she just let herself stand there, admiring Tam's angled, dark face, his ice-fern eyes, his jaunty smile. She thought of the kiss he'd given her last night and wondered what it would be like to repeat it.

Or to simply take his hand and lead him back into her bedroom, forget all the pretense of courtship and play and ask for the relief and ease of sex. They were adults. Would that be so terrible?

But she was too vulnerable, too tired to contemplate such an idea just this minute. "Would you like some coffee?"

"What, my breakfast isn't waiting?"

She grinned. "Thank you for your help." Heading for the kitchen area, she said, "Have a seat. I'll feed you."

"Not necessary," he said, but he sat at the counter on a bar stool anyway. "I'd love the coffee, though."

She pulled the coffeemaker out and started to take the basket out to put a filter in it.

"Wait," he said, and pointed to the teapot covered in a quilted yellow cozy. "That's tea, is it?"

"It is. Would you like that better?"

"Please."

She poured a mugful and passed the sugar bowl toward him. "Milk?"

He nodded. "You make a good cup," he said. "Unusual in America."

"My grandmother was fussy about tea. She'd spent her girlhood in England and liked to drink good, strong, English-style tea with milk."

The sound of engines retreating came through the

closed door, and Tam stood up, frowning, to peer out the window. "What was that about?"

"Reporters. My sister in Manhattan called me to say Claude's been a big topic of gossip." She sighed, feeling the tension in her neck again. "I'm so tired of all of this," she admitted. "If it weren't for the wolves, I'd just go, start over somewhere else."

"Speaking of wolves," he said. "That's why I'm here. I saw wolf tracks this morning and a blood pool where maybe a rabbit or something was killed. It was over by Orchid Pass. The prints looked like they were headed back this way."

A brightening bloomed in Desi's chest. "That's not far!" Setting the kettle on to boil for a second pot of tea, she turned and picked up her cell phone and punched the speed dial for the caretaker's cottage. No answer. She hung up. "Alex is probably feeding the wolves. I'm sure if he sees Fir, he'll give me a call." She sipped her own tea. "What were you doing up there so early, anyway?"

"Snowshoeing," he said, but something about his expression became shuttered.

Desi trusted her instincts. "What were you really doing up there?"

His eyelids flew upward. He met her gaze, and his mouth took a sheepish little downturn. "I had a dream about her. Seems it might have been somewhat real."

Desi smiled. "I've had lots of dreams about dogs and wolves, Tam. I think they're very good communicators. You picked up her messages. Thank you."

"Ta," he said with a wave of his hand.

A swoop of tenderness moved in her chest. He tried to hide it, but he had that rare and endearing need to care for the small and the weak and the broken. Surely that was what had turned him into a firefighter. "After we have our tea, we'll head up to the sanctuary and see if Fir has made it back."

As they headed out into the morning, Desi tried to ignore the rush of pleasure she felt being in Tam's company. He made everything seem…more, somehow. Brighter, more dazzling, more delicious. Sunlight had moved with gentle lemon juice washes over the snowy hills as the two humans and three dogs headed up the hill to the wolf sanctuary. Tecumseh took point as always, his head high, his speed fast. Crazy Horse, with his border collie tendencies, herded them from the rear.

Tam chuckled at the dogs. "They're a smart lot."

"I'm insanely in love with them," Desi admitted. She kept trying to ignore the shape of his thighs in dark blue spandex, but lime-green piping drew her eye back again and again. He was as fit as an ad in an outdoor magazine.

"Are we going to pass the hot springs?" he asked, looking around with a puzzled expression. "It was round here, wasn't it?"

"It's not right on the main path," she said, "but, come on. I'll take you there."

She veered into the trees, feeling a little giddy. Which made her chatty. "In the summertime this is very beautiful," she said. "Green and lush, with about a million wildflowers. The hot springs mean the ground is a little warmer, so we get some things growing that are not all that usual for the area."

"Yeah? Like what?"

"Um. Well, truth is, I don't really know which ones are which. That was Claude's arena."

He grinned down at her. "I see."

Through the cold green shadows of sheltering pines came the sound of water and the mineral smell of the water. "When my sisters and I were kids," she offered, "we came to camp up here, and there was an herbal shampoo that was popular at the time. That's what that smell reminds me of, all those girls washing their hair with that healthy smelling stuff."

"And did you have such long hair when you were a girl?"

"No. My mother always made me cut it. When I left home, I grew it out to spite her." She fingered the end of her braid. "It's too long, I know. I should find some style that would be more flattering, but somehow I can't seem to find the heart to do it."

"I hope you don't," Tam said.

Stepping into the clearing by the hot springs grotto, Desi waved a hand toward the jewel of her property. Sunlight streamed down into the bowl surrounded by trees and poked yellow fingers into the green waters, illuminating the depths, setting free an even deeper fragrance of humus and earth and minerals.

"Ah," Tam said with respect in his voice. "It's lovely."

Desi nodded, her hands in her pockets.

Tam took her braid in his hand and gave it a mild tug. "When will you invite me to come swim in it with you?"

A shiver walked down her spine. She looked up at him. Even that—looking *up* at the man—was a pleasure. "When would you like to come?"

He stepped closer and wound her braid around his wrist. "I'm at your command, love."

Her imagination produced a vivid picture of his body, naked, next to her in the water, the swirl of bare flesh against her own nakedness, her breasts free and swishing against his chest, her hair loose in the water, his hands—

She ducked her head, closing her eyes tight against the vision. "Not a great idea. Let's just not, Tam."

"Not what?" he asked quietly. "Not swim? Not... kiss?" His mouth moved very close to hers, and a bolt of something hot and not entirely welcome burst through her.

And yet she didn't move away.

Tam wanted her. Simple, clear, plain. He moved his nose over the side of her head, her neck and he felt the tension in her body, the jangled disparity between her wish for him and her wish to resist him.

"I think," he said, touching her ear with his mouth, "that you like control. That you've been calling the shots for so long you don't know how to let go."

"I do what I have to do," she said, and started to move away.

He caught her wrist, and she looked up at him, her

eyes showing the same slightly hostile warning of the she-wolf. "It's safe, isn't it?"

"What do you mean?"

"If you're the boss, you never have to lose control. You don't have to care." He narrowed the space between them until she was staring up at him. He looked hostile, aroused, nostrils flaring, but stubborn, too. Not about to give in. "I think," he said, "you want someone to take control."

"Don't be ridiculous," she said, and rolled her eyes in the dismissive gesture he'd come to recognize was fear.

He simply looked at her for a moment, gauging his next move carefully. Hands? Yes. With a quick move, he captured her wrists in his hands and moved his body into full contact with her own. The layers and layers of fabric between them did not let him feel much of the shape her body, but her breath caught in an aroused way.

He bent his head and breathed his words over her forehead. "I think you've been waiting your whole life for a man who is as strong as you are, as fierce as you are and as sexual." He flicked his tongue over the edge of her eyelid. "Am I right, Desdemona?"

Her breasts rose and fell in a hurried fashion, and he moved his body in a slow way across hers. She did not answer.

"I think," he said in a low voice, "that you want me to kiss you, that you want my hands and my mouth on you, on your lips and your neck and your breasts. I think you want me to tear open your shirt and see your nipples, hard as pointed little nails, sliding into my mouth."

She made a sound, a soft whimper, and Tam pressed his erection against her. Her face was turned sideways, her hands in his wrists. Slowly he bent his head to her ear and sucked her earlobe into his mouth, and when her attention was absorbed there, when her arms went lax, he quickly shifted both wrists into his right hand and bit her earlobe with a quick, sharp nibble. She gasped, writhing against him, her voice a low whimper.

"Yeah?" he said, and circled her ear with the tip of his tongue. With his now-free hand he opened the collar of her shirt and shoved the fabric away, settling his mouth on her neck, making little sucking kisses there. Across her throat, his hand beneath her collar. "I'm thinking you're aching to have me look, that you know we're going to have the hottest, most intense sex of our lives. Either one of us."

With a quick gesture, he unzipped the jacket she wore, and said, "Look up at me, Desi."

She raised her eyes, her mouth parted. Her lids were heavy.

Holding her gaze, he reached between them and fingered open the buttons of her blouse, then with a quick movement, pushed it open. She gasped. Her breasts, unbound, spilled out.

His head nearly split open. Beautiful, full breasts, tipped with broad, coral-brown nipples that were, indeed, at full alert. His member, already throbbing, leaped in eager delight, and Desi felt it. She moved her thigh, and with the slightest, most delectably inviting gesture, she arched her back ever so slightly.

Tam made a low, guttural noise and bent his head into the softness, skimming his chin, his cheek, his forehead over her softness. When she wiggled a little, not so much in control as that shimmy would have led him to believe, he very, very lightly rubbed the bristles on his chin over one nipple, then the other. She wanted his tongue and he gave it to her, but only in tiny, flickering sweeps. Hot tongue. Cool breath. Lightly bristling chin. Her arms fighting him now just a little. Tongue. Breath. Tongue, breath. A soft sound panted out between her lips. She arched, wordlessly begging for depth—

And he gave it, suddenly, suckling hard, and at the same time, sliding his hand between her legs. She cried out in surprise and arousal and wiggled away from him a little, but he didn't let go, just suckled and swirled, teased and suckled and rubbed, ever so lightly, between her legs. "Tam!" she cried. "We have to—"

He shifted to the other side, repeated the sensual torture. She cried out again, her shoulders straining backward, and he made a noise of his own.

Suddenly Desi shoved him away, and stumbled backward, pulling her blouse closed. "This is a bad idea."

He brushed his fingers over her cheek. "Why?"

"Because the whole town hates me. You don't want to get mixed up in all of that. Because I'm not in a great place emotionally and I'll probably get all needy on you."

"That's okay."

"It's not okay with *me,* Tam. I hate that."

"You're fretting too much, love. I'm not a girl."

"I noticed. What does that have to do with anything?"

"I don't care if people don't like me."

"You have a business to run," she said, shaking her head. "You don't know how insular this town can be."

"Don't I?" He crossed his burly arms. "I'm an outsider, too, you know."

"True. How did you get people to warm up to you so fast?"

He shrugged. "The pub was welcome and it's known I fought the Hayman fire. And it doesn't hurt to be an ex-rugby player. Americans love an athlete, yeah?"

Desi laughed. "I'm not sure how many of them know anything about rugby, but you're right about the rest." She flicked a small pile of fresh snow into the warm green water. "It also doesn't hurt that you're big and gorgeous and have an accent."

He inclined his head. "Never hurts."

Desi glanced at her watch. "I've got to get this day going. Come on, let's get up and check on Fir."

With a gentle gesture he captured her braid. "Not so fast," he said. "Before I move one more step, I'm pinning you to an invitation. When can I come and swim. It'll just be a swim, I promise. And I'll even bring some New Zealand beer, how's that?"

"Tomorrow is Sunday," she said. "It's supposed to snow. Come tomorrow afternoon."

He smiled and let her braid go. "I'll be here."

* * *

Tam felt a wolfish swagger in him as they walked the rest of the way up the hill, as if he were puffing out his chest, his tail high. He had a vision of himself as a cartoon character, waist exaggeratedly small, shoulders and chest and arms oversized, and chuckled inwardly.

Next to him, Desi was makeupless, her hair simply scraped back from her face into a braid and she wore a variation of her plain uniform: jeans and a red ski sweater with a white cotton turtleneck below. Objectively speaking, there was absolutely nothing about her that should have snared him so completely. He *liked* her full lips. He liked her dark, guarded eyes. After some covert evaluation, he thought she was going to look pretty great dressed only in her skin.

But it was none of those things that was drawing him in so much. It was odd, but he liked the way she smelled. He wanted to nuzzle in close to those folds of flesh, snuffling like a dog, and the urge embarrassed him in its elemental directness.

The wolves were howling as they mounted the last hill, and Desi gave Tam a glance over her shoulder. "Something's going on," she said, and smiled. "Maybe Fir has made her way back." Waving a hand, she leaned into a run. "Come on, boys! Let's see what's happening!"

Dogs and woman dashed up the path, and Tam hung back at little, watching. She was not fast or graceful, but her legs were powerful, strength in every line of her body. Necessary for her work with large animals.

When she disappeared around a bend in the path, he halted and looked up at the trees. Over his head. Just that fast, he was in over his head.

His slightly abashed and pleased and bemused mood shattered when Desi cried out, "Tam! Hurry!"

He ran up the hill, feeling the sudden burst of pain in his leg. Desi knelt by the fence, and all he saw initially was the slash of crimson staining the snow. It made him think of the rabbit, and he started to smile, thinking it was Fir who'd dragged her prey back home.

Then Desi raised her ghost-pale face to his and said, "Call 9-1-1."

And he saw that the blood belonged instead to Alex, the caretaker, who lay sprawled and unconscious, obviously from a blow to the head.

Chapter 7

Tam called for an ambulance and police as Desi bent over the youth, tenderly checking him over. "Alex?" she cried. "Can you hear me?"

He didn't stir.

"He's really out," Desi said in despair. "Damn." She checked him over. "His pulse is good. He's breathing all right. He lost some blood, but the snow stopped it pretty fast." She looked around, scowling. "Let's be careful about messing up any prints. Do you see anything?

It had all been tamped down pretty well, and Tam doubted they'd find anything, at least right here. "I'll check the perimeter. Do you want me to do anything else? Bring a blanket for him or something? Feed the wolves?"

"There's a volunteer who comes in at ten. She'll feed them. And, yeah, bring out a blanket." She looked away quickly, put her hand on Alex's chest. "He did not deserve this," she said fiercely.

"No," Tam agreed. "Neither of you did."

He walked carefully along the fence, conscious of the wolves watching him. The big one sat in an alert position atop one of the low wooden structures in the clearing, and Tam fancied he could feel the sharp gaze boring into his neck, as if the creature were tattooing him.

There was no fresh snow, but Tam carefully noted any footprints, anything that looked fresh. Along the repaired section of fence were extra prints, but he thought those were Desi's and his own from the day before. He ducked around the far end of the border, which was nestled more deeply in the trees, and he saw a line of tracks going up the hill. Smallish tracks, a woman or small man. They followed the footprints of a wolf or a dog, and Tam figured they were from Desi following Fir.

As far as he could tell, there were no others. Which only meant they'd used the road. He didn't have the expertise to make sense of tire treads, but surely the sheriff did, even in a little town like this. Alex had nearly been killed.

The ambulance pulled up, lights flashing, siren silent. Tam jogged around the fence back to the spot where Desi cared for Alex. Desi explained that she'd just arrived here and found him. No idea when it happened or who could have done it. Tam saw that she was struggling not to cry, and he touched her shoulder. "Go with him downtown. I'll wait for the sheriff and do whatever else you need done."

"Tam, are you—"

"Sure? Yeah." A murderous feeling was in his throat. "Tell me what to do."

"Just wait for the sheriff."

"What about the wolves?"

She looked at the enclosure. "You can go give the baby some attention if you want. He's in the main building. Lisa will feed the others when she gets here."

Tam nodded, examining her face. A red blotch marked her forehead, and he thought she was fighting back tears. Her life had not been easy these past months. He wished he could build a wall around her, keep her safe. He touched her arm. "Find me later, yeah? Let me know how things are going."

Her nostrils flared. He wanted to move toward her, comfort her, take some of that burden on his strong shoulders, but sensed she would not, in that moment, welcome his overture. Her control was too thin.

"I will," she said, her voice raw. She climbed into the ambulance with the EMT and Alex. Watching it leave in the gilded morning, Tam felt a slight sense of disorientation. How could something so evil arrive on such a beautiful day?

Against his hip, his cell phone rang. He carried it simply for the sake of safety when he ran or snowshoed in the backcountry. He didn't recognize the number on the screen and answered roughly. "Tam here."

"It's me, Desi," she said. "I left my cell phone

on the counter of my house. Will you bring it down the mountain?"

"Yeah, sure." He frowned. "How'll I get in?"

"It's not locked," she said. "And don't lecture."

"No," he said. "I won't."

"Look around for Fir, will you? And you can feed the baby if you want. There's pureed meat in a yellow bowl in the fridge."

"It's done," he said. A well-fitted SUV with police lights on rocked up the drive, and Tam said, "I have to go now. The sheriff is here."

Desi sat in a chair covered with orange faux leather and examined the lines in her palms. The life line, thick as a rope and unbroken from top to bottom. The love line—hahaha—jagged and looped until it hit the middle of her palm. The child lines along the outside—one, two, three. Fat chance of that. She and Claude had tried and tried and tried. She had desperately wanted children, and the tests had shown nothing wrong with either one of them, so it must have been some psychological issue.

Don't think.

She refocused on her hands. The knotty knuckles. The short, functional fingernails. The broad palm.

The doctors had taken one look at Alex and rushed him into the mysterious recesses of the hospital. His family all lived on the other side of the mountain, but she'd called them on the way down. Helene was his aunt—or something. She wasn't quite sure. Alex called Josh his uncle and Glory his cousin, but sometimes those were looser designations than they were in the Anglo world.

Anyway.

In the background played a television. Dancing mops skidded over a sparkling floor, and Desi glared at it with annoyance. What inanity! Who could care about such things?

The front door to the clinic swished open and two deputies, dressed in the Mariposa County official green, came in. Desi was relieved to see her nemesis Gene Nordquist was not one of them. One was Jimmy Rineheart, with his bowling ball belly. The other was a glum-looking man with eyes like a basset hound. Desi couldn't remember his name, but he'd been kind enough to her when she was in jail for several days last November. She stood up and shook their hands.

Jimmy raised a thumb toward the emergency room. "I'm going to see what I can find out from the medical folks," he said. "Be right back."

Desi nodded. She hoped he brought back some real news about Alex's condition. A ripple of dread moved through her belly, and for a moment she thought she might be sick. Sitting down, she said to the other deputy, "Did you talk to Tam?"

"Is that his name, the Australian?"

"He's a New Zealander."

"You don't say." Basset Hound's gold tag said Deputy-Sheriff Brian Moore. He opened a notebook and flipped it until he came to a page thick with scribbling. "Need to ask you a couple more questions, if you don't mind, Ms. Rousseau."

"Doctor."

He raised doleful eyes. "Pardon me?"

"It's Dr. Rousseau," she said.

"Oh, sorry." He settled beside her, his long legs making her think of a grasshopper ready to spring. "You found the boy this morning?"

"Yes."

"Did you hear anything overnight?"

"Not at all."

"Does Alex have any enemies?"

Frustration welled in her. "No. He's really a good kid. He has family all over town and the rez. He works hard. He has a steady girlfriend. All that stuff." She took a breath. "It wasn't about him. Someone wants my land. They cut the fence yesterday and one of the wolves escaped and now this."

The deputy nodded gravely, looking down at his paper. She noticed he didn't write anything down. He'd already got this much. "Thing is, we don't really know what to do, Dr. Rousseau. There's not much evidence we can use to track your vandal."

"So, I have to just live with this? Alex could have been killed!"

"No, no. I'm not suggesting that at all. I was thinking more like—" he rubbed his nose "—maybe you need to install some cameras."

"Oh! That's a good idea, Officer Moore." She pressed cold fingers to the top of her eye. "In the meantime, do you think there might be enough evidence to show there's harassment and I might not be the one who killed my husband?"

He blinked. Slowly. "You think it's all related."

"Yes."

"Well, you'll have your day in court. Soon, isn't it?"

"Not that I know of," Desi said. A point of contention, that they still had not officially charged her, nor cleared her. Her lawyer insisted it was better to leave it like this for the time being, and selfishly, Desi wanted to be part of her sister Juliet's wedding before the trial took place. If she was convicted of Claude's murder—however wrongly—she wouldn't get to weave flowers into Juliet's hair on her wedding day.

Now that *would* be a crime.

Rineheart was on his way back down the hall, his hat pushed back on his high forehead. Desi stood. "How is he?"

"He's awake. Groggy, furious, but awake."

Desi pressed her palm to the hollow of her throat. "Thank God."

"Looks like he's going to be all right, but sounds like they're gonna have to send him into Denver for observation, make sure nothing's wrong."

She nodded, but her heart sunk. "Poor kid."

"He says he didn't see anything. He heard something—though he keeps saying the word in Indian, so I don't know what he means—and went out to see what was going on. Never saw a thing."

"And you didn't find anything?"

Jimmy looked apologetic. "There's so many footprints up there, Desdemona. Can't tell what's yours and what's an outsider's, particularly with all the melt and tromping yesterday with the fencing."

"Maybe I *will* put in some cameras."

"It would be a good idea." He touched his hat, in preparation for leaving. "There's more to this than I'm currently understanding, but I'm thinking these folks aren't playing games. You're in pretty serious danger."

"I can't leave the wolves."

"I know. Maybe you can hire some more body-guards or something."

Desi found a wry smile. "Wolf guards. Hahaha."

He smiled, too. "That's right, sweetheart, never lose your sense of humor."

"I'll do my best."

Desi had already alerted Helene that she'd be late. Once she spoke to Alex, and made sure he had family to fly with him to Denver, she headed out into the mild winter morning. The streets were thronged with the ski set in their brightly colored clothes and hats. The omnipresent sound of the lifts swinging their way uphill and back down, over and over and over, rumbled beneath everything, a sound Desi noticed only now and again.

She crossed the street near the Black Crown and headed up the hill to Helene's house, thinking she hadn't thought of a way to tell Tam to reach her. Surely he'd just take her phone to the pub and she could go get it later. She didn't have his cell phone number.

But—maybe Lisa had arrived at the center by

now and she could reach him that way. She'd call from Helene's.

And call the judge. Wincing, she rubbed her forehead. Too much to do. Way to much. How could she keep going like this?

Helene, a Mariposa Ute, opened the door before Desi could knock. A lean, rangy woman with hard-carved features and the large, all-seeing eyes of a sage, she and Desi had been friends nearly from the time she'd arrived in Mariposa.

"Come in and tell me how my nephew is doing. Is he okay?"

Desi recounted what she knew. "His mother was there when I left."

"Good." Helene waved her into the kitchen at the back of the house, which smelled of oranges and fresh pancakes toasting on a grill. "Come in, sweetheart. I made a plate for Glory, who insisted she was going to die if she didn't eat, but I waited for you."

Desi smiled. Touched Helene's shoulder in thanks. Soon she would be Juliet's mother-in-law, technically a relative of Desi's, as well. And Josh, gentle Josh, who was so good to her sister, would be Desi's brother.

Sitting at the table, her feet swinging in pink tennis shoes, was Glory, Josh's five-year-old daughter. A stunning child with soft walnut-colored skin and a black braid falling to her hips, she was direct, eccentric and absolutely adorable. "Hi, Auntie Dez!" she said. "I'm sorry I couldn't wait for you. I just got too hungry."

Desi bent and kissed the part in her hair. "That's all right, sweetheart." She sat down at the table. "Have you seen my sister this morning?"

"She had to work," Glory said. "But she's supposed to come get me after lunch."

Juliet had been working on creating a shelter and legal office for immigrant women who came, mostly with husbands or boyfriends, to work in the service industry in the ski areas. Housing, food, child care and the social ills of struggle were ongoing problems, and Juliet had proven to be very good at negotiating solutions. One of the hotels had been convinced it would be to their benefit to set up a child-care facility for the hotel maids.

Helene said, "Finish up your breakfast, baby, and you can go play."

"I know, I know," Glory said with a sing-song tone. "Adults have important things to talk about."

"You are just too old for your age, you know it?" Desi said.

"Well, I'm not *stupid,* you know."

"You're precocious," Helene said as she tossed droplets of water on the grill. They sizzled off, and she ladled pancake mix on the griddle. The scent of baking dough sent long fingers into Desi's empty tummy, and it growled.

Glory shoveled a last forkful of pancakes into her mouth, drank her milk and wiped her face clean with a cloth napkin. "I'm done."

"What do you say?"

"May I be excused?"

"You may."

When she'd left the room, Desi said, "I need to hire some people to guard the perimeter of the land and especially the wolves."

Helene settled across the table, her long fingers covering Desi's hands for a moment. "You look tired."

A clutch of tears caught in Desi's throat, and she looked down to hide it. Helene's hands tightened gently, her fingers cool and strong. "I am tired," Desi said. "It's been one thing after another."

"What have you been doing to rest, hmm? To take care of yourself?"

Desi shook her head and had to admit the truth. "Nothing."

"This is the season in which we are meant to rest, go underground, sleep more, so we can be ready for the spring when it comes."

"I know," Desi said, and raised her eyes. "You're right."

Helene reached up and brushed a lock of hair out of Desi's eyes, a motherly gesture that made Desi's chest ache with the honor of it. She'd had little kind attention from her own mother, and Helene's abundance of nurturing felt like falling out of a gloomy, dark day into a sunny one.

She'd originally met Helene within a month of arriving seven years ago, when the Ute woman approached Desi in the grocery store and asked if they could share a pot of tea—Helene's modern-day version of offering a pipe to a stranger. Desi had agreed. Helene had explained that for many years, she had been holding sacred sweats for women on what was now Desi's property. It was a very special place, with clear, cold water running in a stream to the east, the hot springs in the south, the mountain to the north and the old burial ground to the west. Without hesitation, Desi had agreed to allow her to continue. In time they had become friends. In time Helene had taught Desi the traditions associated with sweats and invited her to join the small band of women.

One of the teachings Helene tried to impress on the women who—no matter their background— tried to do too much, was to respect natural seasons and cycles, in nature, in life, in the body. Winter was meant to be a time of rest and quiet. Which was hardly how Desi had been spending it.

Sitting in Helene's kitchen, all the pressure of the outside world dropped away, and Desi felt as if she could be herself with the figure of the great mother that Helene embodied, mortal hands and mortal brown eyes and warm, husky mortal voice giving body to Mother Earth.

"I feel so lost," Desi admitted quietly. "I don't know how to keep fighting this. I don't know why I should have to—how did I offend the universe to bring so much down on my head?"

"There is a lesson in everything," Helene said. "We do not always know why things come to us to be addressed, but we usually do know what is required."

Desi bowed her head.

Helene tightened her hand on Desi's. "It must feel overwhelming, with so much at stake. The land, the wolves, your freedom, the life you have worked to create."

"Yes." The word was a whisper.

"I know you are tired, child, but you have been honored to be chosen to protect that special land and those special creatures and that holy ground. You are a powerful warrior, and the ancestors will help you."

Humbled, Desi could only grip Helene's hand.

"Now," Helene said, "let's eat and you can keep up your strength." She stood up. "And I'm going to call my brother to see if he can find some strong young men to come help you protect that land." She punched numbers into the phone and held the receiver to her ear. "Can you pay?"

"Sure. The going rate. No problem."

Helene winked, and said into the phone, "Paul, I need about five strong young men to help patrol the wolf center and make sure nothing more happens up there for a while." She listened for a minute and gave Desi a thumbs-up.

There was one errand that absolutely could not be neglected this morning, no matter what else was going on, and that was Desi's trip to see the judge. She stopped by the pub to see if Tam had come down the mountain yet, but no one had heard from him. She considered asking one of the employees who were curiously eyeing her to call Tam's cell phone and was—suddenly—too shy to do it.

Which meant she was sans phone and sans transportation and the judge wouldn't care. If something mattered, he always said, it *mattered*.

So she tromped over to the building that housed Juliet's offices, a square, cinder block office building from the fifties, with white paint on the outside that needed freshening and tiny rectangular windows tucked high under the roof. Inside the waiting room was not as packed as usual. Only a handful of women, ranging in age from about 16 to 60, sat dully waiting in the chairs that lined the room. Spanish language television played from a small set on a rotating stand in the corner. Children played with a table full of Legos.

Desi stopped by the receptionist desk. "Hi, Delores. Is my sister in?"

Delores, a plump woman in her late twenties, with hair as shiny and thick and long as ribbons, nodded. "She doesn't have anybody with her. You can go back."

Juliet looked harried, sitting behind a gunmetal-gray desk, her hair twisted into a knot at the nape of her neck, wisps sticking out at all angles. "Hey, Desi. What's up?"

"Where is everybody?" Desi asked.

"Commodities day."

"Ah." Monthly, the county gave away foodstuffs like cheese and peanut butter and cornmeal to anyone who could prove they lived below the poverty line. "I came to see if you'd let me borrow your car for a few hours." She explained the situation, and before she finished, Juliet pulled the keys from her purse.

"I promised Glory I'd pick her up after lunch, so be sure you get back by one at the latest."

"Of course." Desi bent and kissed her sister's forehead. "You okay? You look tired."

Juliet widened her eyes. "I am tired, but that's all it is. Don't worry."

Desi hesitated. She wanted to ask Juliet's legal advice, but she didn't want to burden her, either. Juliet was planning a wedding, starting a practice and going to counseling for a rape she'd experienced two years ago. And now she was worried about Desi's murder charge. It seemed like a lot for her sister to deal with, and Desi didn't want to add to it.

Juliet caught the expression on Desi's face. "What?"

"What?"

"C'mon, Desi, don't be coy. You want a favor and you're worried about burdening me."

"How do you always know what I'm thinking?"

"Hmm." Juliet put her finger to her pretty red mouth and rolled her eyes. "Maybe because I've known you your entire life?"

"Right. Here's the deal—I need to get an injunction against the people who just bought the land next to mine. They want to open a spa, and for obvious reasons, that's not going to be good for the wolves."

Juliet raised her eyebrows. "Or the Mariposa Trail," she added. It was a pilgrimage route that attracted thousands every year.

"Good point!" She nodded enthusiastically. "I think the main angle is the hot springs flow. They want to use the springs to build a pool and sauna and all of that, and it will compromise the flow to the hot springs in town and all up and down the mountains."

Juliet pursed her lips. "Is that a true concern? And if it is, how did you get away with building a pool?"

"My pool was already there— Nature built it. Or at least the Indians did, a long time ago. It wasn't as elaborate as it is now—we put in the grotto and the rocks, but it was the same basic size."

Juliet pulled over a pad of paper and jotted down several notes. "Okay. I'll have to do some research, maybe pull some county documents, but once I know anything, I'll get back to you."

"Thanks, sis."

"No problem. Now get out of here and let me get my work done so I can have the honeymoon I dream of."

"Done." Desi dashed out of the office, feeling a little more cheerful. Maybe things would work out after all. One step at a time.

Desi drove east, away from town and into the wider end of the valley, where the judge had his farm. It was a miracle of ecology. Alexander Yancy had been raised on a farm in Mississippi in the forties, and he'd used the model of the old-fashioned fields to create a self-sustaining organic landscape. Every year, only about half the fields were planted with fresh crops, which were themselves highly diverse, including herbs that replenished minerals and were then sold to high-end organic distributors. The same field was never planted twice with the same crop. Cows and goats grazed on fallow fields. They fertilized the fields they grazed. Chickens ran free and fertilized their areas and were fed natural grain from the fields the cows had fertilized. Orchards with apples and peaches boasted some of the sweetest fruit on the western slope and the organic honey taken from the beehives the judge maintained on rocky ground that could be used for nothing else was highly prized.

In all, it was a business that grossed millions every year and was growing exponentially as mainstream grocery stores and other suppliers embraced organic products.

The judge, a lean man with grizzled white through his remaining hair, was carrying a bucket of something from the barn when Desi arrived. He looked up curiously and waved when he realized it was she behind the wheel of the little four-wheel drive Juliet had purchased when she decided to sell her Hollywood condo and stay here.

"Hey, girl," he said happily in his thick, drawling accent. "I was beginning to wonder if you were ever going to make it."

She kissed his weathered, nutmeg cheek. "Sorry. If I told you everything that's happened over the past twenty-four hours, you'd never believe it."

"That's all right. You're here now. Want something to eat? Or maybe some coffee?"

Desi felt as if she'd been doing nothing but eating the whole day. "I appreciate the offer, but no thanks. I just had some breakfast with Helene." She glanced surreptitiously at her watch. "Let's take a look at Lacey, shall we?"

The judge's nose twitched. "Well, I might have told a fib about that, Desdemona."

"A fib?"

"You want to come sit with me for a minute, on the porch over there?" He pointed to an enclosed sunroom surrounded with snow and looking inviting with pink geraniums blooming within. "I've got something I'd like to talk to you about."

"Sure." She grinned and punched his arm lightly. "You didn't have to fib to get me out here, Judge. I'm always happy to come see you."

"I appreciate that." He gestured with a large hand for her to go in front of him. When they were both settled in the warm, humid room, he said, "This'll be a bit of a surprise, I reckon, but just hear me out, all right?"

A sudden ripple of worry moved through her. *Uh-oh*. What was this about?

"I've been doing some research, Desdemona, to see if we can get you off on a technicality of some kind. The case is circumstantial, of course, except that little problem of Claude's blood on your clothes."

"We had a fight that morning! I mean, a knock-down, drag-out fight. I had to have stitches, and he got a split lip. Half the town saw it."

"I know that. The trouble is, half the town also heard you tell him you were going to kill him."

The tight pain in Desi's temples, born of too much stress the past two days, rolled into a hammering slam. "What are you saying?"

"There are three things you need, to make a case for murder—motive, weapon, opportunity. You have all three. Blood ties you to the victim and it's well-known you had opportunity. I think you're in trouble if this goes to trial."

"But how can they convict me?" Desi protested. "I'm innocent."

He spread his hands. "Unfortunately, it happens all the time."

Panic rose in Desi's throat as she imagined herself behind bars for the rest of her life. She thought of herself pacing, pacing, pacing, her hair going gray as she yearned for the forest, for a place to run—

She put her face in her hands. "I can't stand that."

"I know."

"And what about the wolves and the land?" She gritted her teeth. "No. That's not going to happen. I won't let it."

"I have a suggestion," the judge said, and cleared his throat.

"I'm listening."

"Marry me."

Desi wasn't sure if she heard correctly. "Pardon me?"

"Marry me," he repeated.

Chapter 8

"Marry you?" Desi echoed. "Like a *wedding?*"

"I know it sounds crazy, but that would mean together we own nearly half the western slope of the valley. Very few Mariposa citizens—from which the jury would have to be drawn—would want to challenge that."

A wave of seasickness moved in Desi's chest. "Judge, that's a very sweet offer, but I—"

He waved a hand, scowling. "Don't dismiss it just yet."

She snapped her jaw closed. Looked at him.

"I know I'm an old man—"

"It's not that!"

"—and you haven't been widowed that long, but

a man gets lonely, Desdemona. And there aren't so many women I'd be able to put up with, or who would put up with me. I reckon we're a good match."

"Judge, I—" she began.

"Oh, we don't have be intimate right off, though I expect I'd hope we could come to a mutual agreement in time."

Desi's cheekbones felt suddenly burning hot. For the second time today, she focused on her hands, her palms, the lines for love and life and children. The air grew thick and she struggled with some answer that would not offend him.

The trouble was, she'd always sort of known he was attracted to her. Unlike some men, he liked her sturdy size, her strength.

And she had used that attraction to her advantage, hadn't she? When she was stuck in jail and the whole town turned against her, she'd sent Juliet and Josh out here to petition for her release. He'd managed to do it, too, and she had no doubt his influence with her case could keep her out of jail.

What good would it do the wolves if she went to jail, after all? The land would be sold. The wolves would be sent to various places. Farmed out. The house would fall to disrepair. All her dreams would be in ashes.

And yet, it wasn't right to use someone for such an end, either. She raised her eyes. "You know how much I respect you and love you, Judge. And I'm honored by your proposal."

He stood up abruptly, knocking the ottoman to

one side in his haste. "Save the rest, Desdemona. I understand."

"No," she said, "sit back down, please, and listen to me."

He turned, slightly abashed, and did as she asked. "My apologies. I'm just a little embarrassed."

"Don't be." Desi reached for his hand. "The truth is, I'm so mixed up and confused and under so much pressure that I wouldn't feel right accepting this proposal. I have no idea what's in my mind."

"That's fair, I reckon. Does that mean you'll think about it?"

Desi wanted to say yes. She wanted to hedge her bets, make sure there was a backup to her plan. But slowly she shook her head. "I'm sorry, but no. I don't see that I'd ever feel right doing that."

His face shuttered and he took his hand away stiffly. "I see."

"Judge, you know I care about your opinion and I would never want to hurt your feelings."

He held up a palm. "We don't have to say another word."

But Desi had a sinking feeling that she'd just taken one step farther into the sucking quagmire that had become her life.

When Tam arrived at the Black Crown, the news crew that had been on the mountain earlier was filming a segment in front of his bar. Eyeing the leggy beauty with a raised brow, he turned on the charm. It would be good for business to have the bar featured in a news story. "Why don't you come in, cuz? We'll buy you a beer."

"Will you answer some questions?"

He unlocked the front door. "Will you ask some about the bar?"

She lifted a shoulder. "All right. Tell me about the bar."

He grinned and flung the door open, inviting the pair inside. "As you see, we're a sports bar. Rugby plays on every set." He flipped the tellie on, and a re-hash of a Brazilian game was on.

"Did you play?"

"I did." He gestured toward his Blacks shirt, hung in a position of honor over the bar.

The cameraman looked around his equipment. "You played for the All Blacks? You're not that fire-fighter, are you? The smoke jumper who nearly got killed dragging all those guys out of the Hayman fire?"

Tam swore internally, wondering whether it would be better to lie or tell the truth. "I was a smoke jump-er, yeah," he said, deciding on a middle ground. "One of my mates was killed in the Hayman fire."

The reporter looked very intrigued. "No kidding. I remember that story. You got some recognition or something—keys to a city or a medal or something like that, didn't you?"

"I'd rather talk about my pub."

"What about Desdemona? You want to talk about her?"

Tam raised his eyebrows apologetically. "Not really."

Undaunted, the reporter said, okay, "How about the skier? Christie Lundgren. They say she comes in here all the time. That she was here the night Claude was killed."

The light on the camera flipped on, blazing white halogen, and Tam scowled. "Yeah, that's right. Christie was here. It's a matter of public record."

"She around anywhere?"

"She's skiing the Olympic circuit, love."

"Ah." She plucked a peppermint off the bar and unwrapped it. "So she is. Now what about Desdemona? You two seeing each other?"

"That's personal, and no I won't answer any questions about her." He started taking stools off the bar. "Can I offer you a cup of coffee?"

"No story here," the woman said, using a cutting motion at her neck.

"Now, that's where you're wrong," Tam said. "There's plenty of stories going around. The wolves up there, for example. There's no where else for them to go if Dr. Rousseau goes to jail for a crime she didn't commit."

"How do you know she didn't commit it?" the reporter asked. The camera was rolling again.

"I didn't even know her then," he said. "Another story you might want to do is about her sister, who's got a whole organization going, to help the people who come in to staff the hotels and restaurants. And there's no place for them to live in Mariposa, so they set up tent villages and trailer parks in abandoned lots outside of town, but that offends the upscale types, so they're moving them out. Do a story on that."

"You know," she said in a voice that was throaty and strong, "I'd love to do those stories, but my boss sent me down here for the sensational story and that's what I have to cover. Indian artist murdered by his wife, and a famous, beautiful skier is the third member of the triangle. Great stuff."

Tam narrowed his eyes. "What if it had been your husband?" he asked.

"What do you mean?"

"What if your husband had been unfaithful, then he was murdered and the whole world was talking about you?"

The woman shrugged. "It's nothing personal."

"Dr. Rousseau has suffered enough," Tam said, folding the bar towel carefully. "Don't drag her through all this."

"New is news," she said, and spun on her heel. "I'm staying at the Centennial Hotel if you change your mind." At the door she paused. "And just so you know, I'm not the only journalist there. Because of the art sales, the story broke on AP two days ago. I was just the first one here."

Great, thought Tam. That was all Desi needed. He made a stab at shifting this one's attention, however. "You want a story on something with substance, I gave you some ideas. And you're welcome to come back and eat if you're hungry later today."

They left, and Tam started the work of opening the front of the house. The kitchen staff had been here for hours, and he popped his head in to say good morning and find out what they had planned for a special. The smells of a bleached sink and roasting pork and freshly cut onions perfumed the air, a scent so redolent it eased away any lingering annoyance with the reporter. "How's it going, mates?" he called as he came in.

Oscar, the level-two cook who followed the main chef around like a pup, had onion tears streaming down his face, but he said, "Fine, boss. Fine. We found you some whitefish for fish and chips."

"Yeah?" he came around the cutting area. "Just remember to use stale old grease," he said, clapping the boy on the shoulder. "Even better, for my tastes, if you let it lie under the warming table for a bit." He headed into the office, and spent an hour entering figures into the computerized books and inventory system. Inventory losses had cost his grandfather thousands every year, and Tam had resolved to be sure he kept up. As he finished, he was whistling under his breath—February looked to be his best month ever, in spite of having to train new staff in three stations and the resultant overtime.

"Boss," cried Amy, "somebody here to see you. Name's Desi."

The center of Tam's chest bumped, like somebody had jabbed him with an elbow. Anticipation? Excitement? Worry? What? He sat back and threw his pencil on the desk. Curiously he rubbed the place on his breastbone and tried to sort it out…. All of the above, along with some hunger and curiosity and good old lust.

"Tell her I'll be right out," he yelled back and stood up, smoothing his shirt in front, running a hand over his short curls. All felt okay.

He found Desi sitting at the bar, a tall lime-green drink in front of her. Her face had not a scrap of makeup and her cheeks were pale, half-moons of darkness showing beneath her eyes. Her posture was defeated. "Well, you look like you lost your last friend," he said.

"I might have," she said, and sighed. "I don't want to go into it, but it's been a terrible morning."

"How's the boy?"

"Alex? He woke up and they took him to Denver. They think he'll be all right, but they want to keep a close eye on him for a few days."

"Makes sense." He took a tall, slim glass from the bar mat and filled it with ice, then cola and squeezed a lime in it. "Did the deputies come to see you?"

Desi nodded. Springs of hair wafted around her ears, touched her brow. "What did they do up there?"

He shrugged his disappointment. "Nothing much. Took a cast of the tire tracks. Looked around, made notes."

"I think they're pretty disappointed, too. Whoever is doing this is being very careful."

"Or they're professionals."

"Good point."

"You look done in, girl. You want something to eat? You want to go home? I'll drive you."

"Don't you have to work?"

He cocked a brow. "That's what I've got staff for."

She nodded. "Then yes, I'd love to go home. This is all just driving me nuts and I need to figure out some answers."

"I'll drive you and help you, then."

"It won't take long," she said. "You can drop me off."

Tam smiled and put his hands on the bar. "I have a better idea. Why don't you let me make a care package to take up the mountain, and we'll tuck it away in the fridge for later."

The cocoa of her eyes turned liquid. "And what will we do in the meantime?"

"You'll show me the hot springs."

"Will I?"

He nodded, watching the secretive dimple flash in her cheek. "Yeah. Then you can catch me up on all the things that have gone on today, and I'll catch you up. Two heads are better than one—maybe we'll come up with some ideas together."

The smile that emerged was reluctant, slow, but very winning. "See, here I am, knowing that you're a big charmer, that I should leave you alone, that you say the same things to all the girls and what am I thinking?" Her gaze was frank.

Tam met it, feeling his nostrils flare. "What's that, love?"

"That I don't care." She picked up her glass of limeade. "Go gather up your tools of seduction, Mr. Neville, and let's get outta here before something else shows up to ruin my day."

"Tools of seduction?" He grinned. "I do like the sound of that." As he headed away from the bar, however, he remembered something else. "First, come with me. I want to show you something."

Quizzically, she raised her eyebrows.

He took her hand and pulled her to the back of the bar and opened a door that led to some stairs. "Go up. I'm going to tell the boys in the kitchen some things, then I'll be right there."

Her expressions said she didn't remember his maps, but she would see them when she got there. "Trust me. Go."

Desi ascended the stairs with a feeling of tense resistance. She didn't really want to go up to his lair. She didn't want to deal with anything. She just wanted to go home.

But the stairs led to a space that made her halt and catch her breath. It was wide-open, with long, double-hung windows on three sides and a gleaming kitchen at the back. Bookshelves were packed with every conceivable kind of book—big, heavy coffee table books, paperbacks by the hundreds and carefully shelved hard-covers that had been well tended. It was not the collection of a man who moved around a lot—too much weight.

Here, too, she was swamped with a recognition that he was from elsewhere. A framed photo of an unfurling fern hung in a place of honor on the walls, and there were sculptures representing a style of carving she associated with the South Pacific, which of course, New Zealand was, though she'd never really realized it before.

But the reason he'd sent her up here was obvious. With a soft gasp of pleasure Desi moved toward the wall away from the windows, where a series of antique maps hung. Magellan's journey. Marco Polo's. Cook's. On a table beneath the maps was a thick book—maps of the explorers—and a globe. A shiver walked up her spine.

Tam's footfall on the stair alerted her, and she turned with a grin. "I'm enchanted. I'm plotting terrible thefts."

"Amazing, isn't it?" His fingers hovered over the journey of Marco Polo, in the late-thirteenth century. "They had no idea what was out there, and they climbed in their ships and sailed away."

"So brave. I wish I could have done that."

"Me, too." He smiled gently. "Sounds like we both have, a bit. You wandered with the Peace Corps, yeah? And I've been wandering, too, all over, until I found this place."

Desi nodded, a thick loss in her throat. "I thought I'd found my home when I came here," she said, and it was impossible to keep the sound of sorrow out of her voice. "It's devastating to find out I didn't."

He put his arm around her. "Things will work out." He gave her a squeeze and let her go. "Come on, now, let's get you home, yeah?"

Desi looked at him. "Yeah. Thanks."

By the time they reached Desi's cottage, every bone in her body was exhausted and aching. For two solid days the bad news had been coming and coming, and she wanted it to stop—even for one afternoon.

And maybe, she thought, looking overhead at the gathering clouds, she would get her wish. Surely if it snowed, everyone would just stay inside and mind their own business.

"Bring all that inside," she said to Tam, who lugged a bag of groceries and a cooler full of mysterious foods he'd taken out of the kitchen of the Black Crown. The weight of it made his bicep bulge against his long-sleeved T-shirt.

She noticed that he was limping, too. "How bad did you hurt that leg of yours?" she asked, lifting her chin toward it as she took her own bags of supplies out of the back of his truck. The dogs, alerted by the engine, came racing from behind the house, tails high, happy barks ringing into the still forest.

"Dogs," he said, laughing. "Gotta love 'em."

Desi bent over and let each of them give her kisses in turn, then headed for the cabin. "No dodging the question," she said.

"Pretty bad," he said. "Spiral fracture. Landed badly in a parachute jump. It was a bad day."

She opened the door and led him into the kitchen, feeling the same mix of pleasure and pain that she felt every time she came into these rooms. She loved the light spilling through the windows and the smooth handiwork of the wide boards of the pine floor and the faint, lingering scent of woodsmoke.

But Claude had laid the floor and fitted the windows. Desi had sanded and varnished the counters, the sills, the doors. Every molecule of the building was mixed up with Claude.

She dropped her stuff on the chair. "Let's get dressed to go up to the springs."

"Not just going naked, eh?"

"You wish."

"You bet I do." His phone rang and he glanced at it with a frown. "Sorry, I have to take this. It'll be quick."

Desi waved a hand.

"Hello, Zara," he said into the phone, and pointed toward the fridge with his free hand, gesturing to show he wanted to put the food away.

Desi nodded and turned her attention to putting the groceries away. Nothing fancy. Powdered hot chocolate. Cheese, bread, cider, pears—wildly expensive and out of season, but Desi didn't care today. A person deserved a treat now and then.

Behind her, Tam seemed to be using an exaggeratedly calm voice, as one would with an unreasonable teen or cranky five-year-old. She wondered what children he knew.

She wondered if he wanted children of his own, and flushed at the thought.

And yet—it was impossible not to imagine all kinds of things with Tamati Neville, with his big strong body and capable hands and kind heart. If she were a wolf, she'd be circling him intently, responding instinctively to the good genetic material presented by him. Were humans really so different? Wasn't she responding to Tam, in part, because he was good father material, both genetically and in terms of his character?

A little voice in her head said, *Nice try, Rousseau.*

Because she'd been forced to be honest with herself this past year of upheavals, she recognized the authentic sound of that voice. While it might very well be true that on some level she was responding to Tam as father material for her unborn children, the bottom line was she just wanted him. She wanted to see his body naked. Taste his strong neck, run her tongue over his Adam's apple and the little patch of hair just below his lip.

He kept talking to the person on the other end of the phone, giving Desi an apologetic expression. "Zara," he said, "I've really gotta go. I've got things to do." He listened a minute longer. "Right. Call the numbers you have for the doctors. Get out and take a walk. Don't sit and brood. And I'll see you in a few days, yeah?"

Desi tried not to eavesdrop, but there wasn't anyplace to go. From the tone of the conversation, she thought it sounded like he was a rescuer. Uh-oh. Maybe that was why he liked her, too—she was in trouble and needed rescuing, or at least that's how he saw it.

She'd just have to prove to him that she was perfectly capable of taking care of herself. She'd been doing it all her life, thank you very much.

The tinny voice spoke a single sentence, and Tam hung up. "Sorry about that," he said. "I'll explain, but before anything else comes up, let's get our butts out of here and up to that pool, yeah?"

"Agreed."

By the time they hauled their towels and late lunch up the hill, the sky was thick and dark, the color of a gray crayon. There was no wind, and as Desi stood by the side of the pool, trying to psych herself up to take off her coat, she said, "It'll be great once we actually get in."

"Only one way to get there." He sat on a big red-granite boulder and started untying his shoes. Desi watched, suddenly shy to take off her own protective layers. Her bathing suit was modest, as were all her clothes, a tankini with plenty of coverage, but it was still embarrassing to take off her coat and yoga pants. She kicked off her boots stripped off her socks and waited for Tam to turn around.

When he reached for the hem of his purple fleece, to pull it off over his head, she was going to slither right out of her pants and wade into the water, at which point she could shed the coat. But the best-laid plans "oft went agly," as Burns said. Hers went.

Because Tam caught the hem of his T-shirt, too, and pulled both fleece and shirt off in one smooth motion, leaving his torso clothing free.

His beautiful, muscular, tawny-skinned torso.

Bare.

And instead of taking her clothes off, Desi simply drank in the sight. The powerful rounds of his shoulders, his smooth biceps and broad chest, scattered with only the smallest bits of jet-black hair. His belly wasn't a six-pack of vivid abs, but there was only a thin layer of flesh over the muscles beneath. Around his arms were circles of abstract art, tattoos that emphasized the size.

She must have made some sound, because he raised his head and gave her a smile.

"Wow," she said. "You have a beautiful chorso, er...test." She closed her idiotic mouth. "Chest," she finally managed, but even she had to laugh.

Which broke the ice. Tam wiggled his eyebrows. "I have high hopes for yours."

"No comparison," Desi said. She bent and skimmed off her yoga pants and put them aside, not as shy about her strong, muscular legs as she was about her upper body. She carefully hung the pants in a tree branch. "We might get fresh snow," she said. "You should hang things high."

He nodded, turning to put his shirt and sweat jacket on the tree, which showed off his long, powerful looking back. Desi availed herself of the moment to zip out of her coat and dash for the warmth of the pool.

"No fair," he said, grabbing her arm. "I've got one bad-looking leg. If we're going to be shy, how'm I gonna get in the water without you looking at it all up and down?"

Desi halted, looking up at him. "Oh, sure. Like this is fair! I'm plump. You're scarred. Here's the difference—the world loves scars, not bellies."

"Can I tell you something?" He looked down into her eyes, his thumb running over her arm, which was getting cold.

"If you make it fast."

"Get in, and I'll tell you in the pool."

"Deal," Desi said, and waded in, using steps cut

into the side of the hill to go deeper into the water. She and Claude had worked on this, too, but somehow, she didn't think of him so much when she came here. She found her favorite perch, on a flat bit of slate sticking out just right and settled in. "It's great!" she cried.

"Give me a second," he said, and she saw that it was no easy thing for him to get out of his jeans. One leg was much weaker than the other, and he finally kicked out of them and bent over to pick them off the ground, taking a long time to stand back up again.

He wore boxer shorts, striped in lime and forest green, as cheery as he was, and they fit loosely. Desi realized she was staring again and turned her eyes demurely downward, looking at her legs in the fragrant water, little white sticks far below the surface.

As if on cue, snow started to fall in fluffy little flakes. Tam climbed the embankment and stood at the edge of the pool. "Do I jump?"

"You can. It's not that deep."

"Or?"

"Just wade in gently. There are some kind of steps on the wall."

The stiffness did seem to be causing him some difficulty, and Desi was ashamed that vanity could keep her from giving him help. She peeled away from her perch and held up a hand. "Step in, and I'll help you."

From this angle, she could see the mess that was his left leg. There were ragged scars high on the dark thigh and crisscrossings of tiny white lines over the knee and shin. It didn't move well. "Did you shatter the knee?" she asked as he captured her hand.

"Among other things," he admitted, and came down into the water beside her. Their legs brushed, their forearms, too, and for one long moment, they were very close.

Tam's hand came up under her chin. "I'd like to kiss you, Dr. Rousseau." His thumb brushed her lower lip. "But I think we'll stick with our earlier deal."

"Deal?"

"Your move."

"Oh. That." Nervously she gestured toward the edges of the pool. "Let's, um, sit for a while and get warm, shall we? There are rocks set into the wall, if you want one."

"Kay-oh."

Desi moved to her underwater perch, lifted her chin in the direction of his leg. "What other things?"

He found a stone alongside the wall and settled comfortably, water up to his chest. "Shattered knee, shattered ankle, spiral fracture of the femur." He gave her a rueful grin. "No more smoke jumping for me."

"What happened? Do you mind talking about it?"

"No. It was just one of those bloody bad-luck landings. We hit the spot, but a blast of wind caught the fire and it shifted direction as we were headed down. The updraft caught me just right and knocked me bloody sideways and I landed in a tangle of boulders. My buddy, Roger, covered me with a fire blanket and headed out for help, but there was a—" he cleared his throat and touched it, as if the words were sharp rocks "—burnover that knocked him down and he was killed."

Desi moved instinctively toward him, put her hand on his shoulder. "Tam, I'm so sorry. I didn't mean to open a wound."

He gave her a smile, only slightly forced, and put a hand on her hair. "Don't worry, love, I'm over it." He put his hand back into the water, and Desi eased away a little, letting the current create a cushion of safety between their bodies. "But that phone call I got at your cabin? That was Zara, Roger's widow. She's not over it."

"And he saved your life at the expense of his own, so you feel obligated to care for her," Desi guessed.

"Not a big leap, eh?" He shrugged as if he were embarrassed. "Maybe it's kinda stupid, but I feel I owe her."

"I didn't mean that," she said, and smiled. "It's part of your personality, isn't it?"

"What, being nice?"

"Not just that," Desi said. "You're something of a rescuer, I think. You take care of things. People." She inclined her head, smiling at him. "You rescued that baby wolf, you went snowshoeing to try to rescue Fir, and here you are, being kind to me and bringing food and keeping the world at bay for me. That's even what you do for a living."

"D'you mind?" His pale green eyes showed earnestness.

"No," Desi said, and realized she meant it. "It feels good. Thank you."

"No trouble," he said with a wink.

"Just don't go around thinking this is how I live, Tam. In need of rescue."

"I believe you." He raised his head and there was a sober expression on his face. "But we need to talk, yeah?"

"About?"

He moved toward the edge of the pool and snagged a can of soda for himself and tossed her one. "Let's brainstorm this business with all the threats and problems you've been having. When did it start?"

Desi popped open the can and took a long swallow of very good cream soda. "Quite a while ago," she said finally. "Before Claude was killed, I was finding dead ravens on the porch. I remember because I thought it was him, harassing me."

"And it's been ongoing? Or sporadic?"

Desi had to think about it. "Very sporadic. Maybe three groups of harassment at different times."

"Do you have a theory about who's doing it? Why?"

"I don't know. Not as much of a theory as I'd like. I do believe it's all connected. That whoever killed Claude is also the source of the harassment, and I'm pretty sure it has to do with the land."

"Just for the sake of argument, what if they're not related? The murder and the harassment? What if somebody is trying to drive you off the land, but somebody else wanted Claude dead?"

"Okay. So?"

"So let's think about them one at a time. Who'd have a reason to kill Claude?"

Desi took a breath and blew it out. "That's a pretty long list."

"Humor me, love. Who's on it? Besides you."

"Ha ha, very funny." Desi paddled a little, the scents and steam and warmth of the water doing their work to relax her. "Okay, if we start with women, there was me and Christie Lundgren, who was in your pub when the murder happened. I think he was having an affair with someone else before that and dropped her to be with Christie, but I never really figured out who it was."

"Any suspicions?"

Desi said it aloud for the first time. "The dentist's wife. Alice Turner. But that's just a guess. He didn't usually go for that kind of woman, you know what I mean? She's so intense. He seemed to like earthier women."

"I can see that." He narrowed his eyes. "So, I have a conundrum."

"Which is?"

"I don't know how much information you want. How much you knew or didn't know before you split."

Desi hardened her gaze. "I know he was a genuine bastard for about three years before we actually split up, that there were a lot of women. I didn't include them in this discussion because I excluded anyone who seemed to be more than a year before he died. Maybe I shouldn't?"

"He used to meet a woman at the pub sometimes. Dark-haired, with a European accent of some kind. German, Austrian, something like that."

"Renate Franz," Desi said. "She's an art dealer from Aspen. He sold her a lot of work."

Tam met her eyes, seemed to consider. "They had a couple of pretty serious fights. I think she was more than an art dealer."

"Like what?"

His smile was gentle. "Like lovers."

The word hit Desi's being like a cold shock of water. She stiffened and blinked and tried to think of some way to arrange her face into a normal expression but couldn't remember what a normal expression would feel like. Out of the corner of her eye, she saw snow collecting in the tiny hollow of a dead leaf, and against her back, the current swirled, and she had no idea why it should be so shocking and strange to hear of another lover Claude had known when he'd had so many.

But there it was. It shocked her. It hurt, too, in all sorts of idiotic ways. What she wanted to do was weep or howl or at least think of something to say so Tam wouldn't keep looking at her like that, with such dark sympathy in his eyes.

"I'm sorry," he said.

Desi gave a laugh that sounded false, even to her own ears. "Don't be silly. What difference does one more make?"

"Obviously some."

"Oh, I'm used to it. They do keep coming out of the woodwork." She waved a hand, looked up toward the floating snow and let it fall on her hot face, cooling her eyes. "Don't worry about it."

Then Tam was beside her. "Desi, he was an ass, but I was being an arse myself by telling you. Maybe I just wanted your attention."

She looked at him. His beautiful green eyes were very close, his well-cut mouth only inches away. Against her upper arm, she sensed his chest with the crisp little hairs scattered across it like the garnish of a polished chef who knew he was a creature worth the devouring.

All at once she was tired of never asking for what she really wanted, and with a single, smooth gesture, she turned toward him, let the water buoy her up toward him and touched his strong jaw.

He didn't move. "Desi, maybe it's—"

"Shh." She touched her thumb to his lower lip, watched the short, worn nail make an indentation in the firm flesh. "We don't have to keep talking. We can just let things be, can't we?"

"You don't have to prove anything, Desdemona," he said, and his voice was rough as he raised his hands to her face. At his touch, a rush swirled over her skin, down her neck to her shoulders, over her breasts, into her lower belly.

She swayed toward him. "I don't want to prove anything," she said. "I just want to touch you." Her fingers traced the hard muscles of his forearms and she gauged his strength with the expertise of long experience with bone and sinew and tendon— Tam could pick her up and fling her across a room.

Around them, the water bubbled quietly and snow fell in thick, quarter-sized flakes that didn't immediately melt when they touched his smooth brown skin. One star caught on the hair over his right nipple and she leaned forward to flick it into her mouth. Another fell against his collarbone. Another on a bicep. She licked them away, one by one, taking a moment to gauge that muscle with curious hunger, using the tip of her tongue to trace the vein that ran upward toward his shoulder. Her fingers curled around his elbow.

Tam let her explore. He sucked in his breath when her lips closed around his nipples, when she traced a spiral over the middle of his chest. His hands tightened in her hair, but he let her go at her own pace.

And it was oddly, deliciously narcotic for her. His skin tasted warm and spicy and clean, the textures smooth and rough, pointed and sharp and always, always solid. He was as strong and solid as a tree, unmovable. Unshakable.

She raised her face to look at him, and he bent to kiss her, dragging her body close to his. His mouth, hot and full, captured hers and his thick, strong tongue plunged into her mouth, sucking hers out into a dance of erotic grace, the tip of his tongue sending hot shocks down her throat, into her nipples, and she made a soft sound.

A lover, yes. This was what she had been needing. His hands on her back, their bodies floating close together, brushing softly.

Instinctively Desi wrapped her legs around his waist, her body floating lightly against his at first. Beneath her calves were the strong rounds of his muscular buttocks, and she couldn't help putting her ankles against him, to feel it. He made a low, warm noise in his throat, and his hands slid down to her own bottom and with a single, smooth gesture, he pulled her floating body into the thrust of his sturdy and quite fiercely aroused member. There was a lot of it, and he knew just how to move, and Desi grasped his shoulders, let him push his tongue hard into her mouth and push himself between her thighs.

Desi felt a simple, pleased laugh in her throat, and she lifted her head to look him in the eyes. "Well, well, well," she said, and her voice was throaty. The water lent her grace as she rubbed against that sturdy pliance, which was as big as the rest of him, and—

His hands gripped her bottom, and then suddenly he froze. "Desi," he said. "Don't move fast, but turn around slowly."

Sensually dazed, Desi wasn't sure what he was talking about and it took her a moment to reenter the world and look over her shoulder.

And there, panting on the edge of the pond, was Fir.

Chapter 9

"Fir!" she said quietly. "Hey, honey!"

The wolf quietly woofed and turned toward the hill, jerking her head for Desi to follow. "I'm sorry," she said to Tam with a grin, touching his shoulder. "She's not going to sit around patiently and wait."

"Will you come back?" he said.

"Come with me. We'll go back to my cabin later."

He took her hand, carried her lips to his mouth. "Will we?" he said. "Or will you run away?"

She kissed his throat. She reached down into the water and caressed his arousal. "No way I'll be going anywhere. Don't put your tools away, all right?"

His teeth flashed. "Maybe for a minute or two, yeah? But you can open the box anytime. Or maybe—" his fingers found the heat between her legs "—that would be *your* box." He wiggled his eyebrows.

"Ooh, that's—" she made a soft noise of pleasure and surprise "—vulgar here," and gasped a little at his touch.

"It's vulgar in my world, too," he said in a husky voice, his fingers moving steadily. "Nothing wrong with a little vulgarity, eh?"

Desi purred at his touch and sucked in a steadying breath. "Fir needs me." She eased away, kissing his nose. "Soon, soon, soon."

His eyes said he didn't believe her, but there wasn't much he could do. Releasing her, he took the towel she'd put on the embankment for him and waded out of the water. Desi followed, shivering.

Fir stood at the edge of the trees, tail down, eyes alert as she waited. Desi struggled to get her clothes on damp skin and finally just gave up. She tucked her feet into her boots and wrapped the towel around her waist and stuck her arms into her coat. "Lead the way, sweetie!" she said. "I'll meet you up the hill," Desi said over her shoulder. "Do you remember how to get there?"

He nodded. She could tell he was disappointed, and when he emerged from the water, the boxers sticking to all the parts of him she'd felt against her, she felt a ripple down her spine. Longing. Fear. Desire.

But the wolf was insistent. She trotted down the hill and took Desi's hand gently in her mouth, tugging at her. Desi laughed. "I'm coming, I'm coming!"

They dashed through the trees, the small she-wolf

running adeptly through the snow, disregarding the path Desi tried to find. Snow got inside her boots and her legs were cold and she hoped she wouldn't run into anyone in her weird attire, but it was all worth it when Fir crashed through the trees and let go of a howl. In the distance her adopted pup gave a yip, and Fir agitatedly nudged Desi toward the gate.

When they were through, she took the pup out of the inside kennel where they'd been keeping him warm, and Fir nudged him happily all over, then— as she'd been waiting to do—regurgitated the food she'd killed for him.

Desi stepped back, heart in her throat. That was why Fir had gone—she'd been hunting! The pup mewled in gratitude, and Desi felt tears in her eyes.

Behind her, Tam came in. "My heart's breaking."

"Thank you," she said, turning to look up at him. Dampness curled his hair even more, and his black lashes were spiky, framing the pale green irises, a color that should have made his eyes seem cool and instead was always imbued with great warmth and honor and integrity. Had she ever met a man with integrity before?

"For what?" he asked.

Desi shook her head. "Let's go have supper, shall we?"

"I like that idea." He took her hand in his. "I'm ready."

Fastening the door to the kennel so that Fir and the pup were safe again, she headed outside. But as they stepped on the porch, she heard the sound of a truck approaching, and she frowned. When it came around the bend, she swore under her breath. "I have to go get my jeans on properly," she said. "Handle this. I don't know who it is, but at least you have your jeans on."

"You're wearing a bathing suit," he said.

Desi gave him a look. "Exactly."

She dashed back into the cabin and struggled into the jeans, fighting with damp fabric over her wet rear end, and finally got them zipped. Outside, she heard car doors slamming and voices. Several voices, low, their tone a cadence she associated with Indian men. Throwing her coat on properly, she rushed out.

And grinned. Gathered around a worn pickup truck were five Ute men, three of whom she recognized. The stocky, barrel-chested man with the thin, long mustache of his ancestor, Chief Ouray, was Helene's brother Charles, soon to be Desi's relative by marriage. He nodded at her. "How you doing, Desi? Helene said you were having trouble."

Desi danced down the steps and took his hand. "Yes! I'm so happy to see you!" She greeted the others, three young men and two middle-aged. "I've had so much trouble with vandals, and now I guess you heard what happened to Alex."

Thunderous expressions crossed several faces. "I talked to him a while ago," said one of the younger men, a slim hard-faced youth of twenty-two or twenty-three. "He's doing okay. But I'm mad."

"Me, too, Daniel." She turned and drew Tam into the group. "Do you know each other?"

They nodded. Shook hands.

Charles said, "Why don't you show us what you need, Dez, and we'll let you get on with your day. We'll take turns, two each night, eh?"

"Good."

They worked out details of pay, rotation and Desi showed them the cabin. At one point Tam touched her arm. "I'll go get supper hot, yeah?"

She nodded gratefully. Only when he headed down the hill toward her house did she let go of a breath. Men did not always like a woman who took charge—as her mother had so often told her. They liked to feel in charge and in control. She looked at Tam's retreating back and realized that she was looking for signs of stiffness or resentment. She didn't see any.

But then, she hadn't seen it with Claude, either. He'd seemed to be very happy at the reversal of their roles—she the primary bread winner, he the nurturer.

Except—she frowned—he hadn't been much of a cook, had he? Or a housekeeper for that matter.

"How far out does the land go?" Charles asked, stabbing a brown finger into the map on the wall.

Desi brought her attention back to the problem at hand. It didn't matter if Claude had been threatened, or if Tam was. She had a job to do. The wolves needed her, and they never cared if she was an alpha.

To Tam's surprise Tecumseh, the white wolf-mix, followed him down the hill, and they found Sitting Bull on the porch, watching out for things, his nose in the air. Crazy Horse, the big red mutt, trotted over to Desi.

Letting himself into the small house, he breathed in the scent in the rooms. A hint of spice and bread and coffee, all dark and warm, like she was. Desire flowed through his veins, low and steady, giving life and energy to his limbs, his organs, his head, his sex. He wanted her in a way he'd not wanted a woman in a long, long time. Maybe ever.

And he was sure that she would retreat, that the interlude with the she-wolf and the Indians, then the walk down the hill in the cold, would bring reason and thoughtfulness to her, make her wary of him again.

A memory of her strong legs looping around his waist flashed over his internal eye, and he could taste her lips, her tongue, as he took out the food he'd brought from the pub. Favorites of his: a pie made of lamb and onion and a thick gravy; fluffy white rolls, made the way his granny made them; roasted carrots. All solid, healthy food for a healthy woman who worked hard and needed her nutrients. It was surprisingly satisfying to feed her.

But then, he had a lot of his grandparents in him, didn't he? As he bent over the oven to see how to light it, he remembered them urging customers and neighbors, Tam and his sister and all their friends, to eat, eat, eat. Piles of good simple food, which gave him the body he needed to grow tall and strong and play rugby.

The flame in the oven caught and he tucked the dishes in to warm, thinking how to recapture Desi. He wanted her in his arms, all night. He wanted to make love, to ease the heat in him, but he also wanted to give her some relief, some sense of protection.

He heard her step on the porch one instant before Tecumseh stood up and went to the door, waiting politely, all fluffy white alertness, for her to come through. When she came in, his tail swept the floor in a dignified way. He licked his lips, and Desi bent down to kiss his nose. Her braid, heavy as an anchor, slid over her shoulder. Delicately, Tecumseh touched her chin with the very edge of his tongue and raised his paw in greeting. "Yes," she said, "I am still here. I still love you." She touched his head and gave Tam a grin. "How does anyone live without dogs?"

"I don't have one," he said.

"Gads, man! Better get on that. I'm not sure you're allowed to live in Mariposa without one."

Tam nodded, but he was caught in the energy or aura or whatever it was that was Desi, admiring the angle of her cheekbone, the fullness of her mouth, pink without painting, the curls springing up along her hairline. "I live above the pub. No place for a dog, that."

"All right, we'll let you have a reprieve, but only six months." She flung her mittens on a table and unwrapped her scarf and hung her coat on a peg by the door. "That smells good," she said. "Do I have time to take a quick shower?"

Tam spread his hands agreeably. "It's only pie and rolls. It's just heating."

"Sounds good." Desi pulled the rubber band out of her braid. "Is there anything else you need? Feel free to look around. *Mi casa es su casa.*"

"How about some tea? I could go for a cuppa."

She grinned. "That accent really is adorable. I'd love some, as long as you say cuppa all the time."

"Cuppa, cuppa, cuppa."

Tugging off her socks, with one toe and then the other, she padded through the kitchen and paused in front of him, putting one hand on his belly. "Are you as nice as you seem, or is this still the charming thing?"

Something hot and painful went through the middle of his chest. He put his hand over hers. "No man likes to be thought of as nice, darlin'. I'm charming, yeah? Let's leave it at that."

"We can do that." She walked into the bathroom and he heard the shower run. Tam put the kettle on, warmed the pot a bit and dropped teabags into it. In the bathroom, he could hear her humming in the shower, and the sound made him wistful. It was a warm and wifely sound, wasn't it?

To escape the thought, he opened the belly of the woodstove and used the poker to stir the embers, then rebuilt it. By the time she got out, her hair wrapped in a towel, it was roaring, and he closed it with a clunk. The kettle began to whistle and she moved to the stove and rescued it, pouring hot water into the waiting teapot.

A little shyly she went over to where he knelt, his hands braced on his jeaned thighs. "It's nice to have company," she said, sitting cross-legged on a pillow. She put a brush down beside her and unwrapped her hair, which fell in long, long tendrils down her back.

He spoke impulsively. "Can I brush it for you?"

"It's hard to comb when it's wet," she said. "How about when it's dry?"

"Did I tell you my hair was once down to my shoulders?"

She grinned. "No."

"It was." He took the brush out of her hand, gently. "I'm sure yours could not be worse."

"All right."

He sat behind her, and starting at the bottom, worked the knots out of the long, long strands. It was curly and thick and healthy. He loved it.

"If you had long hair, were you a rebel, then?" she asked, rubbing the fluffy body of the omnipresent Crazy Horse, who'd flopped down in front of her.

"For a bit," he admitted. "Maori pride and all that."

"Is that when you got the tattoos?"

"Yeah." He thought of himself at fifteen, lost and lonely, isolated at the northern end of the land. "My sister went to college and it was just me and my grandparents, out in the country along the tourist road. I got drunk one night with my friends and got the tats in a parlor where everyone was doing tribals. My friend got his face done."

Desi looked over her shoulder in alarm. "Face?"

He shrugged. "It's not so strange there. Maoris tattoo their faces. It can be beautiful."

"Really? But wouldn't it be—" she hesitated, "sort of antisocial?"

"Maybe, but there are some who think they shouldn't be judged for it. Like Ute men wearing their hair long, in braids, yeah?"

"Right. Still, is it all right to say I'm glad you didn't?"

He smiled. "Yes."

She looked at him again, searchingly. "I like your face the way it is. It's very handsome."

He thought there was warmth blooming between them again, but he left it there to grow. "Thank you." He nudged her to turn around and worked through another section. "In the old days, the tattoos were carved into the skin and stained with dye. Women had them around their mouths. They are passed down from mother to daughter, father to son, a family thing."

"Wow." She stared into the fire's bright orange flames. "I envy you the cultural connection of an ancient way of doing things, traditions, all that. We didn't have any when I was growing up."

"You likely did. You just didn't recognize them. Sunday dinner with pot roast, yeah?"

Desi chuckled. "Martinis at six, and rack of lamb at eight."

"There you go. Which reminds me." He stood up and went over to check on the food. "Lamb pie," he said, "and white rolls and roasted carrots. Ready anytime you like."

She stood, and the magnificence of her hair tumbled around her shoulders, over her full breasts, touching the top of her jeans. Her face was freshly scrubbed, her complexion as clear as a glycerin soap.

In no way was she beautiful, but that did not seem to matter to Tam's sense of pleasure, to the warmth spreading through him. He thought her shining dark eyes, her natural cleanliness, her sturdy strength and thick, long hair alluring beyond belief.

"I'm starving," she said.

"So am I," Tam said, and bent down to kiss her. Again her lips, plush as marshmallows, were a delectable surprise, and he found his hands on her face, cradling the delicate bones of jaw and cheek.

She kissed him back for one minute, then pulled back. "Food," she said, and touched her belly.

He held on to her arms for a moment, then rubbed them. "Don't run away from me, girl."

"Is that what I'm doing?"

"I don't know. Maybe you're just hungry."

She grinned, a genuine, spreading of light across her face. "Maybe."

"It's good food," he said, and touched her nose with the tip of his finger. "Sit. I'll make our plates."

As they were eating dinner, Desi's phone rang. She groaned. "I'm starting to hate this phone. It seems like bad news every time I pick it up." Warily she glared at the screen. It showed a photo of Juliet and her soon-to-be stepdaughter, Glory, mugging for the camera in rhinestone tiaras. Maybe it wouldn't be so terrible.

She flipped open the phone. "Hey, sis. What's up?"

"Did you know there are cameras stationed outside of the Black Crown, and in front of my house and all over town, waiting to ambush you?"

Or maybe it would be that bad. Desi's heart plummeted. "Jeez, I'm tired of this! I'm sorry if it's causing you trouble."

"No problem for me," she said. "I wonder about Tam, though. Is he there with you?"

Desi shot a look toward him. "Why would you ask that?"

"It's been on television, Dez."

"That he's at my house?"

"That he was. That you made breakfast for him."

"Well, I didn't exactly make breakfast for him, but I told them that because I wanted to get rid of the reporter."

Tam raised his eyebrows questioningly. Desi shook her head.

Juliet said, "You did make breakfast for him?"

"No. I mean, I had to have breakfast with Helene." Had that only been this morning? What a long day it had become! "But Tam lied to help me get rid of the reporters who were here this morning."

"Tam—Tamati from the Black Crown, right?"

Desi scowled at her sister's tone. "Yes."

"He was at your house at breakfast time this morning."

"Not like that," Desi said. Though—she met his wolf eyes—he might be tomorrow. She tucked a lock of hair behind her ear and turned slightly away, embarrassed. "He just came to see about the wolf pup."

There was a pause at the other end of the line. Then, "Are you *seeing* him, Desi?"

Over the table, spread with the remains of their very good lamb pie and excellent bread, Desi grinned at Tam. "I'm looking at him right this minute, if that's what you mean."

"You know what I mean," Juliet said.

"I do," Desi replied, "and it's none of your business, little sister."

"Desi, it's too soon. I don't want you to get hurt."

"Juliet," Desi said with exaggerated patience, "again, none of your business. I'm a big girl."

Tam was smiling.

"Whatever. You want to butt into everyone else's lives, but no one is allowed to say anything about *yours*. Did you ever think—"

"What? That I should have listened to Mother and Daddy about Claude, that he wasn't good enough for me, all that stuff?"

"No," Juliet said evenly. "I was going to ask if you ever think maybe I just worry about you?"

Desi bowed her head. "Sorry. You're right. Thanks for your concern, but I'm okay."

"Thank you. Listen, I also called about something else—the injunction you wanted me to look into."

From her plate, Desi plucked a corner of bread. "That was fast."

"It's not a big place, you know. I just called over to the courthouse to do some checking, and I found out something very interesting."

"Tell me."

"There have been some geothermal studies done on the area, including your land. Really focusing on your land, actually."

"I don't understand why that's significant."

"I didn't see the results of the studies, but they could be looking for energy modules or something like that. Maybe you need to have some studies of your own done."

Desi nodded. "Okay. And does it say who contracted for these studies?"

"One is held by a corporation, the other is as you expected, your new neighbor, the developer. His name is…let's see—" there was a sound of rustling papers "—Biloxi."

"Yeah, that's him."

"Hmm," Juliet said, "this is interesting—this name sounds familiar. Franz? Who is named Franz?"

"That's the art dealer from Aspen."

"It's also the name of Biloxi's wife. Elsa Franz."

Chapter 10

"Elsa Franz?" Desi echoed.

Tam's head lifted. "She's a model, just married Biloxi," he said.

A soft headache started between Desi's eyes, and she rubbed the place. "This just gets more and more complicated all the time. What would they have to do with each other?"

"I don't know," Juliet said. "Maybe it's coincidence. Maybe it's not. But it's worth looking into."

"You're right. Thanks, Juliet. You've been a big help. I'll come by tomorrow and we'll talk about your life instead of mine."

"I *do* have a wedding in four months," she said. "Oh, and Miranda called me, by the way. She has actually agreed to wear a bridesmaid's dress as long as it isn't satin. I told her you'd already vetoed it."

Desi chuckled. "I'm glad she's coming."

"Look into the geothermal studies, babe. I think it could be very important."

"Will do." Desi hung up and put the phone on the table. "I'm half tempted to just turn the damned thing off."

Tam pulled his out of his pocket and held it in his hand. "I will if you will."

She met his direct gaze. "Then what?"

His mouth lifted on one side. "Turn it off and I'll show you."

Recklessly Desi picked up the phone and flipped it open and pushed the button. The powering-off song sounded, and she put it aside.

Tam stood up and came around the table. "That's more like it," he said, and held out a hand to her. Patiently.

For a moment she simply looked up at him. His sturdy thighs, planted like tree trunks before her. His broad chest, his strong hand, held out to her. His hard-cut, handsome face—the angles of cheekbone and sensual mouth and the light-struck pale green eyes regarding her so calmly and steadily. Below his lip, that tiny patch of rebel hair that made him look like a rock star or a bad boy.

She wanted him. Putting her hand in his, she stood up. "It's so rare for a man to be taller than me, so much *bigger* than me."

"And for me," he said, pulling her into his body,

"it's a rare pleasure to have a woman who is strong and sturdy."

Desi winced. "Ow!"

One side of his mouth lifted, even as he pulled her close to his body, bringing their hips and thighs and torsos into contact. He was hard as rock, shoulder to knee and the full-frontal contact gave Desi a jolt of almost knee-buckling heat. It had been so long since she'd made love. Had sex.

Whatever. Even the words—*sex, making love, man*—gave her a snapping band of heat over her forehead.

"You were thinking you were a frail little flower, babe?" he teased gently. "Maybe a violet or something?"

"No," Desi said, and lowered her gaze. "But a man doesn't want to be 'nice'—a woman doesn't want to be 'sturdy.'"

His arm looped around her neck, and he bent down to taste her mouth. "I need a woman who is as strong as I am," he said, and again that tongue, hot and thick, nudged its way into her mouth. "I need a woman who is my equal. As you need a man who is yours."

Desi opened, letting him draw circles on the surface of her tongue, feeling her nipples pearl in readiness. She let her hands move upward, sliding over his powerful chest, to his broad shoulders. She kissed him back, feeling something just let go, as if there was a break in some dam that had been holding back the natural flood of passion a woman in her prime experienced.

Tam made a low, male noise and pulled her into the other room, to the piles of pillows and quilts that were nested in front of the fire. "Let's lie down here, yeah?" Without waiting for an answer, he tumbled backward and pulled Desi down on top of him.

For one breath she paused, suspended in a time before she let him in, aware that once she let him take off her clothes she would tumble into another reality, a life that was different from the one she thought she would have. By making love to Tam, she was no longer standing on the edges of the ruin her life had become, but risking the possibility of a new life—and more ruin.

The thought caught in her throat, sharp and terrifying, and she even found her hand flying up to her throat, covering it protectively. How could she do this? Let him in?

As she hesitated, Tam was beneath her, his big head nestled on the pillows, his fine gentle eyes patient, his hands tangled in hers. As she looked down at him, so afraid and so yearning all at once, he took her hand and carried it to his mouth and pressed kisses to her knuckles. "You look so pretty in the firelight."

Desi melted forward and pressed her mouth to his. "So do you," she whispered. "But what if I tell you I'm too shy to be the leader?"

He smiled, and shifted so that she was beneath him. "I'd tell you I don't mind leading." His hand covered her breast, moving in happy discovery, his long fingers gauging the weight and depth of her curves. He kissed her again and laced their legs together, pressing his hips and a fierce thrust of erection against her pelvic bone in the most ancient of dances.

Desi let herself drift in the moment, letting him stoke the fires in her body, feeling blisters of arousal explode from cell to cell, across her lips, over her forehead, gathering in sharp delight in her nipples and belly and sex. His mouth moved over her lips, her chin, down her neck, lazily, and then he paused for a moment and braced himself so he could unfasten her blouse and spread open the cloth. "I've been looking forward to this part," he said in a voice that was a little ragged, and he opened her bra, revealing her breasts.

Gathering her flesh gently and with genuine pleasure, he bent and tasted each nipple in turn. "You have beautiful breasts, Desdemona. I've been thinking about them ever since you came into my bar without a bra."

A shudder moved down her back, and Desi moaned against her will as he drew circles around her nipples, drew the taut flesh into his hot, wet mouth, let go, began again. "That feels so good, so good," she whispered, and pulled on his shirt. "Take off your shirt. I need to feel you, too."

He obliged, revealing taut, smooth flesh, that bare scattering of hair. He pressed down against her, sighing as their chests met and their lips tangled, their limbs.

But Desi was finished with foreplay. "I hope I don't give the wrong impression," she said suddenly, "but I just want you in me. Please."

His laugher was low and soft, and he lifted himself up to take off his jeans. Desi didn't wait for him to take hers, she skimmed out of them, for once not caring that her tummy was not perfect or her arms were not thin. Her thoughts were not on what she looked like, but what he looked like—

And Tam, naked, was worth a moment of admiration. He knelt before her, and when he would have come forward, Desi put a hand on his hard, flat belly to stop him. "Wait one minute," she said, "and let me look at you."

He stopped and let her admire him—the beautiful rounds of shoulders and smoothly muscled chest and belly, lower to the high round of his hips and the powerful, if scarred, thighs. And there, nested in a neat triangle of black curls, the weight of his sex, just now thrusting out proudly. Desi felt another layer of something fall away, and she moved so she could cup his genitals in her right hand and bent to taste him. He put his hand in her hair, making a pleased sound, and said, "Another time, sweet," and pulled her up, then pressed her back again, taking a moment to open the foil package he'd taken out of his pocket. He handed her the condom, and Desi willingly put it in place, suddenly dizzy with the desire to have him in her.

They seemed, all at once, to be one body, one mind, one organism driving toward a single goal. Tam gathered her into his arms and spread her legs forcefully and plunged his tongue into her mouth as he plunged his member deeply into her waiting sex,

and they both made fierce, sharp noises at the pleasure. Desi grabbed him, his hips, and in a panting,
whispery voice said, "Don't move for one second,"
so she could revel in the delirious sense of being
filled, stretched, expanded.

He held still, his mouth moving, and then, slowly,
he began to move, and Desi moved with him.

And it wasn't like anything she'd ever known.
There it was, one minute, sex. Good sex and sex that
she needed, sex with a man who was kind and had
shown himself to be nurturing, but in all, sex, like
food, a thing for the body.

And then, in the next minute, her body was
alight, head to toe and her brain was illuminated,
and some other part of her, what some called a soul
or a spirit, that was illuminated, too, and it seemed
that if she were to weep or sweat, the fluid that
would come out of her would be drops of white
light. Over her, Tam kissed her face, her mouth, her
neck, moving, and she moved with him, and there
was a moment when she thought, *Oh, this is too
much, we're in trouble* and Tam said, "Open your
eyes, Desi," and she did, and so they looked at each
other. He was peering down into her eyes and she
was captured in his fern-soft irises as the energy
between them built and spilled and tumbled them
into another world.

Tam fell against her neck with a sense of being
spun around in a cyclone. He nestled his nose next
to her neck, moving up against her jaw, her body

pliant and warm and quivering beneath his, and he thought, Uh-oh.

After a while they parted and he pulled the blankets over them. Neither spoke. In the quiet darkness, with the fire flickering and cracking, Desi lay on his chest. He threaded his hands through her hair lazily. She traced his tattoos. "What do they draw on their faces, the women?"

"Curlicues," Tam said lazily, his hand drawing slow, small circles on her bare back. "It goes around their mouths, like facial hair."

He could feel her smile against his ribs. "How very patriarchal."

"Yeah. It's traditional culture. Most are, yeah?"

"I guess. Some Native American cultures are matriarchal. Navajo, for one."

"Is that what Claude was? Navajo?"

"Yes."

He thought of a day in the pub, when a raucous lot of hikers had been celebrating the successful completion of their route. Claude had been buying a pair of pretty Germans beers, and chatting with them in what appeared to be very bad German. They kept laughing and teasing him, but another woman at the bar said, "He has a Bavarian accent."

"He ain't no Indian, that's for sure," a Ute man sitting next to her said.

Desi lift her head. "What are you thinking?"

He trailed a lock of her hair through his fingers and considered. He wondered if they should just leave the subject of Claude all the way alone, but eventually they had to figure out who killed him. Every clue counted. "Somebody told me once that he didn't know enough about Navajo culture."

"He grew up in the city," she said. "Denver."

Tam nodded. She waited, stroking the length of his back in a slow, meditative way. "Why would he have a Bavarian accent when he spoke German?"

"As far as I know," she said, "he only spoke English and a little Navajo. Well, and Spanish, of course. We met in South America. He was teaching and so was I."

"I heard him speak German quite a bit," he said. "One of the tour groups that leads hikers on the Mariposa Trail is German, and Claude liked talking to them."

"I see." She sighed, rolling away from him. "God, I was an idiot."

Tam reached for her, pressing a kiss to her wrist. "No, you weren't. He was just a good liar, and you believe the best in people."

"Do I?"

He grinned. "You do. And we're not talking about your bastard of an ex anymore tonight."

"No?"

"No. We're going to have wild sex, over and over and over again."

Desi's eyes went smoky. "Yeah?"

"I'm going to find things out about your body that you never knew."

And though she resisted, he pulled her inexorably toward him, pulling her naked and beautiful breasts onto his naked and smooth chest. The sensation ex-

ploded in about seven places in his body and mind
and heart, and he had the sense to think, again, uh-
oh. But it wasn't enough to stop him from kissing her
again, and then spending three solid hours exploring
every single inch of her body and letting her do the
same to his, until they were both drained and limp
as old clothes, and fell into a deep, dreamless sleep
wrapped in each other's arms.

When Desi awakened the next morning, she
was startled to discover Tam had disappeared. Her
first reaction was painful—a squeeze of disappointment so hard that she felt her heart was being slowly
squished by the left-front tire of a twelve-ton semi.

Then she wondered if he might just be in the bathroom or something. Don't be hasty, she told herself.
But she heard nothing. No water running. No sound
of things bumping.

Nothing.

And come to think of it, if he was still here, where
were his clothes? She turned over, saw piles of dogs,
her underwear, a bra on the chair, her boots by the door,
but nothing that belonged to Tam. He was gone, all
right.

Her stomach rolled. Fooled again.

Damn it.

Then nature insisted she couldn't lie there whimpering about a disappearing man, and she jumped up,
naked, and dashed for the bathroom. Sleepily she
relieved herself and tried not to think about Tam or
being naked or—

A piece of paper was stuck to the mirror.

> Sorry to run, Desi, but I thought it was better to get out in case more reporters might be poking around. You were sleeping so deeply, I thought you deserved the rest. Call me when you get up.
> Love, Tam.

In the tiny room, holding the piece of paper in her hand, Desi thought of her strong emotions upon waking. She thought of the connection she'd felt to Tam last night, that sensation of light flooding her body and mind and soul—

And shuddered. Too much, too soon. She needed to steer clear of Tamati Neville. Way clear.

Bending into the sink, she washed her face with very cold water, letting it clear the lingering heat, the lingering wish she felt for him. Raising her head, water dripping silver from her chin, she looked at herself hard in the mirror. "Remember how it felt at the end," she said. "Don't go there again."

Today, she resolved, she would put her attention on work. Work and the wolves and finding out what the hell was going on with the investigation of Claude's murder and who was behind the vandalism and the attack on Alex. Plenty to keep her occupied, and her thoughts away from memories of a highly erotic evening.

Filling the sink with warm water, she resolved to compartmentalize her thoughts. She was good at that.

On a Monday morning, there would be more than enough work for her to do at the clinic. After a simple breakfast of cereal and coffee and banana, she rumbled down the hill in her big truck bathed in the brilliance of morning. There was something in the slant of light as she came into town—was it spring? There were still piles and piles of snow. They would still have two solid months of skiing traffic before the slopes closed and the trails opened.

But there, angling through a stand of pines in the park at the center of town, was the first long fingers of spring sunshine. It was more gold than winter sunlight, heartier. It gave her a thread of hope, which was quickly doused as she drove into the lot in front of the clinic.

A handful of cars were parked there—the receptionist's blue Bronco, crusted with the red mud that lined the road to her house; a white pickup truck that had a camper shell on the back; two other, smaller vehicles, all local by their plates.

And one gleaming black monster of an SUV with Denver plates. A news crew was set up, filming the circling marchers Alice Turner had assembled, as if on cue. Desi let go of a little roar of frustration as she pulled into the lot and sat with her hands on the wheel for a moment, trying to decide the best course of action.

Maybe it was the relaxation lent her nerves by a long, healthy bout of sex last night—never to be discounted as stress relief—or the simple, pathetic look of the four marching women carrying their pitiable signs, but for the first time what Desi felt was not anger but exasperation, and maybe some pity. What did they lack in their lives that they could make a cause of Claude Tsosie?

And yet there were things that Desi needed to be careful of. Despite the absurdity of the situation, she was under investigation for murder, and the case, though circumstantial, was not exactly smoke and mirrors. It would be best for her to avoid reporters.

The newscaster, this one a man in a white sheepskin coat and blue ski hat and dark glasses, spoke to Alice Turner while the other women marched around and around, poking their hand-lettered signs in the air.

She took a breath and turned off the car. When the news crew spotted her and came running over, she held up a hand. "I don't want to talk to you," she said, but over their shoulders, she pointed at Alice with a fierce look that said, Get off my property.

Alice tossed a smug look her way, but she shuffled her minions off the property and they started chanting again.

The reporter, a fit, good-looking man, said, "Don't you want to tell your story, Desi?"

She looked at him. "No. I have work to do. Please don't harass my patients."

As she turned to go inside, the man said, "What do you know about the geothermal pool beneath your land?"

Desi almost paused, her foot in the air, and turned to ask what he was talking about. But that would be exactly the shot he wanted. With an effort she continued walking, ignoring the question, and hoped the little hitch in her step wouldn't show.

Inside, however, she said to her receptionist, "I need to talk to my sister as soon as possible." She stripped off her coat and hung it in the closet and took out a white vet's coat. "And if you have some time this morning, will you see what you can find on the Internet about geothermal pools or heating— anything like that?"

"You got it, boss." Sasha, a buxom girl with wide blue eyes, handed her a stack of pink papers, an apologetic expression on her face. "Phone messages for you."

Desi sighed. When would this whole nightmare end?

And what exactly had she ever done to deserve it? Headed to the examining room, she flipped through the messages from strangers and friends, most of them commenting on the news stories that must have aired last night on the ten-o'clock news. One was from her sister, Miranda, and it said only, "Call me. Urgent information for you."

It was only then that Desi realized she'd never turned her phone back on after last night. She pulled it out of her bag, pressed the button to power it up, and waited with the phone in her hand while it warmed up. For a moment she wondered if she should go ahead and give Tam a call, let him know she—

What? Enjoyed herself? "Liked" him? What would she say? It was weird that he'd left without saying goodbye. Weird to have to make the next move.

Still, she very nearly punched in the numbers, and

then poked the number for voice mail instead. Maybe he had called *her*.

There was only one message, from Miranda. "Thought you should know Claude's paintings have quadrupled in price in two days, sister dear. You're sitting on a small fortune."

She hung up, thinking about the message that wasn't there from Tam, and his big, toothy smile with the dimple that enlivened his left cheek and that small patch of hair beneath his lip. Did she want to do this? Go through all the courtship rituals, the ups and downs, the excitement and devastation, the hope and the pain? Did she really want to have to decide if it was his turn to call or hers?

Maybe not.

So think about something else.

Through the sunny window, Desi could see the slowly circling protestors, Alice at the helm, as always. What if Alice had killed Claude? She owned more of his paintings than anyone else—except Desi. With him dead, Alice would not only have the satisfaction of getting her revenge, but his mediocre paintings would be worth a lot more.

Alice. Interesting possibility.

Except—Desi sighed—that didn't explain the harassment and ongoing vandalism. Maybe the two events were not connected. Maybe Claude had been killed for one reason and Desi was being targeted by an entirely different entity?

How could she find out?

One thing she did know—nothing in her life

would be all right until she knew who killed Claude. She couldn't have a relationship. She couldn't move forward with her plans for the wolf center and education programs to help serve the wild wolves coming into Colorado. She couldn't heal, really, until the whole thing was resolved.

One way or another, she was determined to figure it out.

Chapter 11

After Tam left Desi sleeping, he drove down the mountain to his apartment, a collection of Victorian rooms above the Black Crown. It had been a run-down apartment when he first took over the building, but over two years time, Tam had gradually transformed it into a wide-open set of rooms with brilliant views of the mountains through the side-by-side sets of double-hung windows all the way around.

He showered the night from his body, thinking that would be that and he'd get on with his day. Below, he heard the first clanging of pans from the kitchen in the pub, and he stood awhile longer, letting hot, hot water beat down on his shoulders, his head, his body.

Desi.

No, she would forever be Desdemona in his mind now. Desi was much too short and simple a name to capture the complex lusciousness that was embodied by the woman.

Embodied. The word gave him sizzling visions of the night before. Her white throat, arching in the orange wash of light from the fire, the curve of her shoulders, the expression of rapture he'd glimpsed in an unguarded moment.

As the silver, hot water ran over his body, he fancied he could feel a ghostly imprint of her fingers running down his spine, clutching his buttocks— He started to get hard. Again. After the energy expended last night, he was amazed. How could there be anything left?

And yet, even as he climbed out of the shower and rubbed himself dry on a thick towel his sister had sent him for his birthday, he felt a lingering sense of arousal, like cobwebs over his senses.

As he fried an egg for breakfast and brewed a pot of his nefariously strong coffee, he wished Roger were alive. Roger, who always seemed to have good insight into the hearts of men—and women. Roger, who would have at least been there to listen, so Tam could sort it out himself.

Carrying his meal to the table in front of the long, high windows, Tam was acutely aware of missing his friend. They'd met at a training course and immediately fell in synch—the same jokes, the same slightly sick sense of humor. As he looked onto the craggy, snowy peaks of the San Juans, Tam mentally offered a conversation.

"Roger, I'm in trouble with this one."

"Yeah, mate? Trouble how?"

"She's too much for me, maybe too broken. A wounded dove. I don't do that anymore."

"Huh," Roger said. "She's strong."

"Is she?"

"Don't be a bastard," Roger said in his mind. "Whatever else you do, be real with yourself and her."

Real.

Tam touched his chest. Real.

He'd been thinking, when he met Desi, that they'd have a little fling. She'd thrown down the gauntlet that very first day, after all, with her comment that she couldn't be charmed. In his lexicon, that meant, "Do your best and I'll do my best to resist." He figured they'd each be the rebound person for the other—Tam rebounding from Elsa, Desi from her murdered—and unfaithful—husband. They'd have a hot, blue affair, then get down to the business of being friends.

Friends. He should have noticed that before. He didn't think of ex-lovers as friends. It was too sticky most of the time, too complicated.

But he *liked* Desi, that was the thing. Liked her company, her beautiful voice and quick intelligence. She was easy to be around. A mate.

Mate.

Friend in American.

Wife in Kiwi.

Damn.

The thing was, it had been electric from the beginning. A man would have to have been blind not to notice her lovely body, the lush breasts and sturdy strength. Not to pay attention to those velvety brown eyes that seemed to offer a luxury of sinfulness to come.

A promise, it turned out, that she'd kept. Had he ever, ever liked a woman's body so much? There was so much to her. The weighty breasts that were round and plush. A softness of lower belly to brace his hips against, a heat to her skin that warmed him all night as he curled around her and awakened to taste a shoulder, the edge of her ear or—

Mate.

He put his head into his waiting palms, thinking there was a foolish thing, that he'd gone and fallen in love with a prickly woman who had more trouble than she knew what to do with and hadn't been widowed six months yet.

With a sense of panic, he picked up the phone and dialed the many numbers to reach his sister in Auckland. She answered on the first ring in her fluting, pinched accent. "Hello!"

"Anna," he said. "It's Tamati. I think I've fallen in love. What do I do?"

"Well, I'm fine, too, love. The weather's fair— we've not had a dark day in a week. You?"

"I'm living in Colorado," he said with a grin. "It's never dark here."

She chuckled. "So, who've you fallen in love with?"

Tam sighed and settled at the table, picking up his cup. And he rambled the whole story out to her—how he'd found the wolf cub, then found Desi, then all the other things in between. He left out the wild sex, but she put it in. "Lust, then, is it?"

Tam scowled. "No."

"Good. You know, Tam, I always thought it would be this way for you, that you were wandering the world so you could find the woman who would be right for you. Will you have big strapping boys for rugby?"

He grinned, thinking of Desdemona's sturdy thighs and big feet. "Absolutely." A sensation of terror went through his middle. "But Anna, I've only known her a few days. Maybe a week. How can I believe she's the one?"

"Trust yourself, brother," she said. "You'll do the right thing."

"Right." He turned the conversation to other things, to her work and her boyfriend and his wish that she should come visit him in Colorado, then he went downstairs to work, checked on the kitchen, the specials for the day and the bar, which was still closed. The containers for coins to support the wolves caught his eye and he suddenly remembered something Desi had said on the phone last night. Franz was the name of the art dealer out of Aspen, the pretty dark woman he'd always assumed had a Polish or eastern European accent.

But Elsa's name was Franz, too. He'd never given it any thought. It could well be a coincidence— it was a common enough name—but it was enough of a coincidence it deserved a little more exploration.

Were the two related? And if so, what was the connection to Claude?

Taking his dishes to the sink, he noticed the time and wondered if Desi would call. Maybe he should call her—but it was still pretty early. He'd let her sleep.

In the meantime, he had a pub to run. He tucked his cell phone in his pocket and, whistling, went downstairs.

Desi kept herself absorbed with animals through the day, and arranged to meet Juliet at her house for dinner. A good dodge, Desi thought, to keep Tamati Neville out of her mind.

Except that nothing was really keeping him out of her head. At lunchtime, she checked her phone messages and was disappointed not to find any from him. At two, she saw that he was in her Caller ID, but he hadn't left a message.

Maybe she should just call him. Like a grown-up.

The thought gave her butterflies, and even when she genuinely intended to call, she couldn't seem to get her fingers to dial.

And it was as if everything conspired to keep him front and center in her mind. It seemed she could smell him in a waft from her sleeve as she put on her coat; that she heard the echo of his flattened Kiwi accent in the drawl of a South African man who brought in his cat for shots; that a little echo of his breath had somehow lingered in her ear.

Good grief, Rousseau, she told herself, scrubbing her hands and arms at the end of the day. *You've got it bad for this guy. Why don't you just admit it?*

But it was just sex, wasn't it? Agreeable, mutual

sex between willing adults. And what sex! He was a master—knowing when to slow down, when to speed up, when to—

Again she caught herself in a sensual thrall, staring off into space as ripples of delight moved down the back of her neck. Drying her hands on the paper towels she took from the hands-free dispenser, she then combed out her hair and rebraided it. In the reception area, the girls were putting away the magazines left scattered around the area. Overnight, a janitorial firm would come in and clean thoroughly, and the techs cleaned the animal areas, but the receptionist and secretary held sway here.

"Wow, it's a disaster in here," Desi said with a chuckle.

"It's always like this on Mondays," Sasha said. "Hang on, and I'll get you what I found on the Internet about geothermal stuff. It's pretty interesting."

"Thank you." Desi accepted the folder of material and tucked it in her battered, soft leather bag. "I'm off now. If you see Alice Turner and her crew on the parking lot, make them move."

"Got it, boss."

At the door Desi paused. "Have you guys been approached by the news people?"

They exchanged a look so guilty that Desi's heart sank. "You talked to them?"

"He was nice," Ellen, the secretary said, but her stained red cheeks gave away the real reason she'd talked to him—he was gorgeous.

"What kinds of things did you talk about?"

Ellen shook her head, looked at Sasha. "Nothing, really. We just said you were a good vet and loved the animals and wouldn't hurt anybody."

That sounded all right. "Uh-huh."

"And he asked about Claude, of course. We said you guys were through a long time before he started messing around with that skier."

Not as good. "Okay."

"And—we told him you were seeing somebody new, anyway, that sexy rugby player at the Black Crown, so you wouldn't care anyway."

"I'm not seeing him!"

Sasha rolled her eyes. "Okay, boss, whatever you say."

"I only met him for the first time like a week ago."

"And I saw you in his truck, and he was looking at you like you were a Victoria's Secret girl he wanted to undress."

Desi sighed. "Don't be so romantic, girls. It's not like that."

"Oh, you deny it? C'mon, Dr. Rousseau—you know you like him. How could you not? He's exactly your type."

That struck Desi like a cold trout. "My type? What do you mean?"

Ellen giggled. "A big, sexy, kind of ethnic guy. Dark and charming."

She must have looked as stricken as she felt because Sasha elbowed Ellen with a powerful arm. "Shut up!"

Gathering up the shreds of her tattered dignity, Desi said, "Well, do me a favor—don't talk to the reporters. Remember I'm under investigation for murder, and they need to hang this on somebody, so you never know what might get me in more trouble. Get it?"

A hand flew up to Ellen's mouth. "I'm sorry! I forgot about that part!"

Desi waved a hand wearily. "Never mind. Just don't talk. See you in the morning, girls."

As she headed out the door, she heard Sasha say to Ellen, "You doofus! You could have got us both in big trouble!"

The door swung shut before she heard Ellen's answer. At least, she noted, the protesters were gone for the evening. Small blessings.

Juliet had cooked one of Desi's favorite meals, a beef stew thick with carrots and potatoes, with a side of biscuits so fluffy they nearly floated off the plate. Glory was home with her father, and Desi was glad— it gave them a chance to talk urgently and privately.

And yet—

"I've barely seen you and Josh together at all the past week or two, Juliet," Desi commented. "Is everything okay with you guys?"

Juliet blinked and said, "Fine!" in a voice that was reassuring. "We've both just been trying to make sure the house is ready and we have our work done so we can have a guilt-free honeymoon."

"Good." Desi buttered a biscuit and spread it with marmalade. "How is the house coming along, anyway?"

Juliet had sold her Hollywood condo for a sub-
stantial profit, and they had invested it in a house
not far from town, on the bus line. It needed some
cosmetic work before they moved in, and Juliet was
sticking to her old-fashioned desire to be married
before they lived together. "Very well, honestly.
The old kitchen is out, and the contractors are coming to put in the floors next week. Barring disaster,
it looks like it should be finished far ahead of the
wedding."

They talked about the wedding, then, and the
dresses—Juliet was letting the bridesmaids choose
their own gowns, for which Desi would be eternally
grateful—and fittings and flowers. When they'd finished their stew, Juliet collected their plates and
poured fresh coffee and took out a thick folder. "I
found out some very interesting things today, sister
dear," she said.

"I had my assistant do some research on geothermal features," Desi said, and she, too, pulled out a
folder. "Not that I've had any time to look at it."

"It's all right. I did have a chance this afternoon to
sort through all the features—there are hot springs, fu-
maroles and geysers and mud pools, and this area has
all of them, except geysers, which are relatively rare."

Desi nodded. "I know there are a lot of hot springs
around here, and obviously, there's a big stream on
my land and running through the area."

Juliet nodded, a frown on her smooth forehead.
She pulled out a sheet of paper. "The thing is, I
couldn't figure out why the hot springs alone would

cause such interest in your land. And why would anyone hire extra geothermal studies to be done when the hot springs are already well-known?"

Desi nodded. "Good questions."

Juliet paused and scanned the papers in her hand. "I think I figured it out." She handed the sheaf to her sister. "Take a look."

The document was an official-looking study, cloaked in geological terms and legalese that made no sense to Desi. "This is practically unreadable," she said with annoyance.

"I think it was written that way deliberately, to knock people off the scent. But it seems to say, Desi, that beneath your land is a very deep, entirely enclosed lake. A *hot* lake."

"Wow, that's kind of cool," Desi said, imagining a pristine pool in a deep cave, steaming and boiling beneath her land. "No wonder snow melts oddly there—and we get some funny growth, too."

Juliet smiled with genuine amusement. "Yeah."

"What?"

"It is kind of cool," she said, "but you're not seeing the big picture and why it matters so much."

Desi shrugged. "No, I guess I'm not."

"It's an energy source, Dez. An endless, undepletable, continually renewable energy source."

"How?"

"It's a fairly rare phenomenon, but evidently the idea is to build a pipeline system that's entirely closed—the water or steam or whatever comes up through a system of pipes, and the heat itself is used to generate electricity, then the cool water is shipped right back to the lake, to be reheated. Never depleted in the slightest."

The implications were astonishing. "That could be worth…" Desi widened her eyes. "Millions!"

"Try billions, Desi. Trillions. It's incalculable."

"And it's under my land."

"Yes. Entirely dead center." She shrugged. "Which is interesting because the Mariposa Utes have been so protective of that land."

A ripple of something moved through Desi's chest. Fear, honor, respect, humility, all washed over her in a tangle of colors and threads. She thought of Helene's comment that Desi had been chosen to help protect this land. She bowed her head and spread her hands in front of her, smoothing the lines in her palms. "What do I do?"

"You don't have to do anything for now, but I thought you should know."

"Right. Thank you. I do need to know this."

"There's one more thing," Juliet said, and she looked apologetic. She passed her another sheet of paper. "The judge was in on it from the start. He ordered the studies to start with."

The judge! "That rat," she said with a growl. "He's always acted like I was so sexy and he was so crazy about me." She rolled her eyes. "I should have known. A man with that much money and power could certainly do a lot better than me."

"Desi!"

She waved a hand wearily. "You know what I

mean. I don't want to get into it, okay? I'm tired and I want to go home and think about all this."

"I can understand that."

As she stood, Desi said, "I heard from Miranda, too, incidentally. Claude's paintings have taken a big, big jump in value, so if you have any sitting around, you might want to put them someplace safe."

Juliet made a sound like a horse snuffling, very ladylike. "As if." She rolled her eyes. "I'd like to dump his paintings in the river. He lied and cheated like a skunk. I hate the way he made you feel about yourself. You don't deserve it."

"Skunks aren't cheaters," Desi said mildly.

"You know what I mean," Juliet said.

"I do." Desi bent down and hugged her sister. "Thanks, sweetie."

"You know that you're beautiful, don't you, Dez?"

"Sure. All five-ten of me."

Juliet pulled back. "Go see Tam. He'll make you feel better."

Tam. Her heart flickered, pinched. But that was her business, not anyone else's. Not even Juliet. "None of your business!" she said, grinning archly to take the sting out of the words, and grabbed her bag. "Thanks for your help and for supper, sister dear. I'll see you soon."

Chapter 12

Tam couldn't remember the last time he'd had such a hectic day. It was one emergency after another from the moment he came down the stairs from his apartment, starting with a leak in the ceiling over the staff room, for which a plumber had to be found immediately.

The bartender for the night shift had the flu—and not just the tequila flu, either; she thought she'd be out for three or four days. Tam's attempts to find replacements were unsuccessful. The flu again. He was looking at filling in at least a shift or two until he could coax someone else into coming in.

And it didn't stop there. One of his best cooks had a fight with a server and walked out. A crate of lettuces proved to be wormy, which meant throwing them out, along with everything they'd been in contact with.

Which meant that the special of the day had to be changed and one of his cooks had to pay the catastrophic prices at the local grocery store for lettuces and other fresh produce.

One thing after another. By late afternoon, he was knackered.

And that wasn't even to mention the news crews lurking around, trying to conjure up a story to send back home so they could stay and ski a bit longer. They kept trying to tease out his connection to Desi, see if they could get an angle. A few liked the rugby angle, and one actually made the connection to the Hayman fire and the smoke jumper who'd been injured, but he didn't want to talk about that, either. He kept deflecting them, trying to protect Desi, his own privacy, Roger's memory.

Too much.

And that, of course, meant that Zara, Roger's widow, should show up. Today. He was startled by her appearance when she came through the door of the pub, wearing jeans and carrying a coat over her arm. She looked thin and frail enough to break at any second, all robin's-egg-blue eyes and wispy blond hair that made her look about twenty, when he knew very well she was close to his own age, thirty-five. There were hollows beneath her cheekbones.

"Hi, Tam," she said sadly, and sat on a barstool. "You said to just come on over if things got bad. They got bad, so I did." She spread her hands. "Not that it seems like they're going that well for you."

He kept his face still and put a rolled napkin with silver inside down on the bar for her. "You haven't been eating," he said. "I'll bring you something. Soup?"

She shrugged shoulders as pointed as the edge of a scissors. "Okay."

Damn. He headed for the kitchen, trying to shake off his annoyance. Saving Tam's arse had put Roger in the grave, it was true, but he was getting a little tired of playing nursemaid to Zara. It had been two years, after all. She needed to find a way through the tragedy and on to the rest of her life.

This, he resolved, would be the last time he let her manipulate him this way. Ladling up the hearty chicken and wild rice soup, with carrots and celery and onion floating in a broth as golden as bullion, he set it on a tray and cut a hefty slice of bread, too.

And if Zara weren't enough, when he returned to the bar, who should be sitting next to her but Elsa, who must have weighed all of fifty-five kilos, but looked as sturdy as a wolf next to the wispy Zara. "G'day, Elsa," he said. "What can I get you?"

"Oh," she said, waving her hand, "just a glass of white wine. I'm waiting for Bill to finish a business deal. Some real estate something or another."

He nodded, fetched the wine for her and a dark, hearty ale for Zara and introduced them to each other. A news crew had followed Elsa—her fame as a model had not died when she retired to Mariposa to find herself a rich man—and they settled at the other end of the bar. "What can I get you, mate?" Tam asked.

The man ordered a beer. Tam waved to the menu, chalked on a scoreboard behind the bar. "We got what you like, mate. Pick one."

"Stella Artois," he said.

Tam filled a couple of orders for servers, rang up some tickets, hustled to the back to fetch more stock for the front coolers and tried to stay away from Elsa's realm. She had that sulky, looking-for-trouble pout he'd grown to be wary of, her perfect chin in her long-fingered hand, her lips plump as raspberries. With her free hand, she twirled a pen around and around.

Let Zara talk to her.

It was only after twenty minutes that he realized Zara probably wouldn't be doing the talking. Tactical error. He headed down the bar to do some damage control, and there was Elsa, leaning close to Zara, who listened, wide-eyed, to what was no doubt a whole load of barely verified gossip. "Hope you're not giving her too much truck, Zara," Tam said with a grin he hoped was winning. "She likes to talk, Elsa does."

Elsa straightened indignantly. "I don't tell lies, Tamati, if that's what you mean."

He raised an eyebrow. "Just embroider the facts a bit, do you?"

The pink lips curled slightly. "Only a little, to make it more interesting."

Zara scowled. "So where's the embroidery in your stories just now? Is this woman a murderer or not?"

she waved to the canister soliciting donations for wolves. "It's been on the news for three days."

A blister of fury burned in Tam's throat, but he glanced down the bar toward the reporter and held his tongue. "The woman is innocent, Zara," he said mildly.

Elsa rolled her eyes. "Tam just wants to think so because he's—shall we say—interested in her." She tossed a lock of long blond hair over her shoulder and cocked a perfectly arched brow. "They found her blood on his clothes. If she didn't kill him, how did that blood get there?"

"Is that true?" Zara asked.

Tam didn't know. He barked, "No," and his fury doubled when Elsa laughed.

"Yes it is. That part is an absolute fact, Tam. It's in the police report."

"How would you know that?"

She smiled her canary smile. "Oh, I just know."

Despite himself, his resolve to listen to nothing she said, his gut fell. Could Desi really have killed Claude Tsosie? Not that he blamed her, but it could put a crimp in any kind of future they might have together. "I don't buy it," he said stubbornly, and headed down the bar to wash glasses.

"Time will tell," Elsa sang out. "Time will tell."

Desi argued with herself all the way down Black Diamond Boulevard. She should just go on up the mountain, tuck in with her dogs and get some sleep. Tam would wait.

If he even wanted to see her, which she wasn't entirely sure about, after all. He hadn't called.

But neither had she.

But she wasn't the one who'd left first thing this morning.

Irritably she made up her mind to let it go, all of it, and put the truck into gear—and then saw there was a parking spot right in front of the Black Crown, which was lit up and cheery like a beacon in the cold night. She was a grown woman and didn't have to wait for a man to call her. She could call him.

Or stop in and say hello.

She had the excuse, after all, of the geothermal studies Juliet told her about. She could talk to him about his knowledge of the subject. Surely he had some ideas, since he'd lived in Rotorua as a boy— one of the all-time hot spots for hot springs in the world, almost as active as Yellowstone.

It wasn't until she'd pulled open the door to the pub and stood just inside, blinking at the noise and lights and music that she remembered she'd never really been a pub kind of person.

But…well, here she was. It would look pretty stupid to turn around and walk out. How did you just walk in and sit down, like you knew what you were doing, when you *didn't?*

And this was a thousand times worse, because everyone in town knew her and probably knew she had her eye on Tam and would be noting their interaction in great detail.

She spied the reporter from the parking lot this

morning sitting at the bar, and mentally kicked herself. What had she been thinking?

Was it too late to turn around and head out?

And yet, maybe it wasn't so stupid. He'd tossed out the question about geothermal features that had finally revealed some answers about what was going on with her land. How had he known? With a new sense of purpose, she headed toward that end of the bar.

It was only then that she spied Tam, behind the bar, talking to two women, both willowy blondes. He was nodding, paying close attention to something one of them was saying—

Get a grip, Desi told herself. He ran a pub. Women would talk to him all the time.

And yet as she crossed the room, which seemed to take ten thousand years, she really saw him in his natural environment. A big, rugged man with a dashingly exotic face and a sparkle in his eye. A man whom women would always find powerfully appealing. Around him was the evidence of his history with rugby and his passion for his native land, in the jerseys hung on the walls and photos of silvery ferns and the New Zealand curlicue.

Before him were two beautiful women, well tended. Very thin. Younger than she, both vying for his attention.

And she was suddenly, fiercely, reminded of Claude, who knew just how to play a roomful of women.

In her mind Ellen's voice said, *Just your type…a big, sexy, kind of ethnic guy. Dark and charming.*

Great. Just great.

Hadn't she learned *anything?*

And if that were not enough, he looked up just then, and Desi saw the exact instant he caught sight of her. He startled, guiltily, and glanced at the woman to his left, a tiny thing with yards of yellow hair.

Desi halted, halfway across the room, pinned by his pale fern gaze that seemed both accusatory and hungry. Standing there in her work jeans, her big hands at her sides, she felt like a cow that accidentally wandered into a field with a bunch of gazelles.

She wanted to turn tail and run. But everyone was watching. This moment would be reported all over the place tomorrow. Squaring her shoulders, she turned her attention to the reporter. A way to save face.

And maybe, if she turned the tables, she could smoke out her enemies and finally be done with this mess. It gave her stride purpose, and she settled down next to the reporter. "Hello," she said, and held out her hand. "Desdemona Rousseau."

He took the proffered hand. "Good to meet you officially. Mick Reed."

Out of the corner of her eye she saw Tam approaching, and took one second to warn him off with a fierce look. He had no trouble interpreting it. He backed away. Desi looked at Reed. "How did you know about the lake beneath my land?"

"I got a tip," he said. "Anonymous."

Desi rolled her eyes. "Please. That's not even original."

He smiled slightly. "All right. I stumbled on something a couple of months ago, about new ways to generate electricity and a particular developer who was being a bulldog about it."

She raised her eyebrows. "Bill Biloxi, by any chance?"

"You got it. When I saw that he'd bought land up here, I was curious. Seemed like there might be a story in it." He pointed to the empty space on the bar before her. "You want something to drink?"

Desi shook her head. "I can't stay. Just tell me."

"What are you going to do for me in return, sister?"

"I'll give you an exclusive—but not tonight. Just tell me what you know."

He measured her. "Not a lot more to it," he said. "I heard about the murder, and your land was right next to Biloxi's and it seemed to me there might be something going on here." He sipped his beer and gave her a wink. "Besides, I like to ski. It's not as though a story like this takes tons of time."

She took a square cocktail napkin from a stack on the bar and wrote her name and cell phone number down. "I'd like to know your sources. In return, I'll give you an exclusive, tomorrow at noon. Fair enough?"

"Absolutely." He took the napkin and tucked it in his pocket. "You won't be sorry."

Desi swung off the stool and headed for the door. Behind her, Tam called out her name, but she ignored him, and by the time she hit the street, she was at a dead run. She jumped into her truck, managed to get it started and was down the street without having to say a word to him.

She should have known. She just should have

known better by now. You could trust dogs. You could trust nature to do what it did.

You could never, ever trust human beings.

With a head-splitting sense of weariness and disappointment, Desi drove up the mountain. Her head actually hurt with a red pulsing anger, the sudden, sharp accumulation suddenly more than her circuits could bear. The attack against the wolf center, then the attack on poor Alex who'd done nothing except take care of the wolves; the reporters, the geothermal studies, the harassment, the judge...

Her cell phone rang but she ignored it. There wasn't anything Tam could say to make that expression any easier to bear. He didn't trust her, wasn't sure about her, and she'd had enough of that.

She'd had enough.

Period.

She drove up the mountain and fed the dogs, then paced irritably for a half hour, wandering from one end of the small cabin to the other, her thoughts whirling.

It had not been rejection of herself as a woman that she'd seen in Tam's eyes, but doubt about her. Maybe her innocence. Maybe—whatever. She didn't care. She was fed up, fed up with everything. She'd come to this place looking for her home, and she believed she'd found it in the kindness of the town's people, in the acceptance Helene had offered.

Then—through no fault of her own, because of the lack of integrity of others—she'd lost it all. Lost the warm sense of community she'd loved. The pleasure of being a respected and honored member of the town. She had belonged somewhere for the first time in her life, and now she didn't and it was infuriating.

And what could she even do?

How could she make them all see that she was the same woman they'd loved and honored? How could she make things right again?

Suddenly she threw her arms and head back and howled out her frustration. Her anger. Her sense of outrage.

Don't you want to tell your story?

With a sharp sense of purpose, she marched right back into the back room where Claude's things were stored, and started hauling them out. The dogs, seeming to sense her hell-bent-for-leather mood, hovered nervously around the perimeter, but didn't get in her way as she carried it all, armload by armload, out to the truck. Armload by armload, she dumped it all in the bed without much concern for damage—clothes and paintings, sketches and pencils and paints.

Her phone rang again. She ignored it.

With methodical precision, she went around the entire house, rooting out the last of anything Claude had put his hands on. The dogs whined softly, and she distractedly patted their heads to reassure them but didn't slow down.

The phone rang. And rang again. She ignored it. And ignored it again.

With a huge sense of satisfaction, she finally took a mop and a bucket of water into the room Claude had claimed, and mopped it with bleach water. The sharp clean smell blotted out everything else, and it felt almost as if she'd been bleached clean herself. Sweaty and satisfied, she stood in the doorway and surveyed her handiwork. Tecumseh whined behind her, his head down, and Crazy Horse nudged his head under her hand.

"What is it, guys?"

Sitting Bull was gone, bolting out the dog door without a sound, and Desi frowned. "What—"

She listened, but heard no cars on the road.

Her phone rang again, just as there was a frantic knock at her door. "Doc!" cried a hoarse male voice. "We got a fire."

And then, finally, she smelled it. What the dogs had been smelling for five minutes—smoke. Thick smoke, wood smoke.

Fire!

She flung open the door, and three wolves rushed inside, yipping and circling. Her dogs joined them, panting, frightened. Charles, Helene's brother, stood there, his face smeared with soot. "It's the cabin at the center," he said. "We called the volunteer firemen, but they're not here yet. You want me to call the tribal police?"

Desi was already picking up the phone. "Yeah. Call 'em. Call everybody." She punched in the speed dial for Juliet, and when she answered, relayed the news. Then she called the number that appeared on her phone history seven times in the past hour. When Tam answered she said, "The wolf center is on fire. I need you."

He said, "I'll be right there."

Desi turned to Charles. "Lock the dog door. I'll bring the wolves down the hill."

"Paul's already bringing 'em," he said in his gruff voice.

"Good," Desi said. "Good."

Chapter 13

After the wolves were carefully settled inside the house, Desi drove her truck to the top of the hill, feeling sick at the flames leaping into the sky above the trees. Who would *do* this?

The little cabin was entirely engulfed by the time she arrived, and despite the volunteer firefighters who had arrived, it was plain it would be a complete loss. Desi huddled into her coat, watching the flames eat the darkness, sparks flying upward—dangerous, but not as terrible with snow on the ground as it would have been later.

In the darkness she finally found Charles, Helene's brother. "What happened?"

His lips turned down, and he shook his head. "Me

and Daniel were walking the fence, and they must've got in here and torched it while we were out. It was just that fast, like a spirit did it."

Desi tried to quell her irritation. She could buy a lot of spiritual ideas, but not a spirit lighting things on fire. "But why would a spirit be mad?"

He shrugged. "Maybe it was a wolf spirit, come to let the others go."

"The only wolves in here are—" she caught his expression "—oh. You're giving me a hard time."

He chuckled, the sound loose and old in his chest. "Yeah." He pointed with one arm to the forest. "Daniel went after somebody. He's a good tracker. Maybe he'll find something, or somebody."

A pickup truck with the Mariposa Ute seal rumbled into the driveway, and Desi recognized Juliet's fiancé, Josh, behind the wheel. The shadows didn't allow her to see who else was there until he climbed out, decked in a fire coat and a hard hat, his sturdy legs carrying him to the perimeter. He carried an ax.

Tam. Of course. She folded her arms as he approached. "You were here?" Tam asked Charles.

"Yeah. No spirits though. A man crashing through the forest. Daniel went after him."

Tam gave the older man a crooked smile, and nodded. "How long ago?"

"Maybe a half hour. Not that long."

He looked over his shoulder. "That's gone up in a half hour?" He pursed his lips. "Somebody made sure it would burn fast."

"You mean, like soaked it with gas or something?"

"Not petrol," Tam said, "because you'd smell it. But something, yeah." His pale fern eyes were impassive as they met Desi's. "They were aiming to scare you, too, without doing any real damage. Snow break there would have kept the animals safe, unless there was an accident or a tree caught fire." He scanned the tree line. "Not likely in these conditions."

Desi raised her eyebrows. "And?"

"They knew what they were doing. That's all I'm saying." He walked away, leaving Desi to stare after him.

"He's your man, huh?"

Desi gave Charles an annoyed glance. "No!"

Charles nodded. "Oh."

Just then Daniel came crashing through the trees, yelling, "I got him! I got him!"

Desi and Charles and Tam ran toward him, Daniel holding fast to his prisoner, a fox-faced man in his forties with badly scarred cheeks. The man stumbled into the clearing and fell.

"'Bout time you caught a break," Charles said, looking down at the man. "Now maybe you'll get some answers."

"I hope so," Desi breathed. "I certainly hope so."

By midnight the excitement was mostly over. The wolves had been resettled, and although they would likely be nervous and noisy for a few days, they seemed none the worse for wear. The fox-faced man was the arsonist, though he had yet to talk about who he was working for. The charges against him were not, at this point, serious, after all. Why spill the beans on a good client?

The county police did agree there was enough danger that Desi required help watching the perimeter until the parties behind the arson had been ascertained and apprehended. Desi nodded with a secret smile when Jimmy Rineheart told her this. *Ascertained and apprehended,* ran through her head for an hour afterward—it was so silly. Why didn't the police speak the way everyone else did?

She was unlacing her boots when a knock came at her door. The dogs didn't even lift their heads, so she knew she was safe with whoever it was, and she assumed it would be Juliet, coming to make sure she was safe.

Or maybe she didn't assume that. Maybe she opened the door because she knew it would be Tam standing there, glowering down at her. "Can I come in?" he said, leaning one hand on the doorjamb.

"What do you want?" she asked.

"Can I come in?" he repeated.

Desi crossed her arms. "What do you want?"

"Where did the blood come from, Desdemona?"

"What are you talking about?"

His mouth looked hard. "They found traces of your blood on Claude."

Desi narrowed her eyes and debated whether to answer or tell him to get lost. Her traitorous body, the infinitesimal cells of her skin and through her body were dancing in anticipation of a party. "We had a fight early in the day. He knocked me down and I even had to get stitches, which Helene will verify if you want her to. Not that it's going to get you any closer to me." She stepped back and tried to close the door.

Tam stuck out his foot and stopped it dead, then pushed inside and grabbed her. Before she even knew what was happening, he'd laid claim to her mouth, kissing her with a fierce, explosive heat that was in no way gentle or kind or even asking forgiveness.

Desi exploded, and they were locked in a frantic, deep embrace, lips and tongues locked in a bruising kiss, her hands on his shirt, unbuttoning it as fast as she could. When she could get her hand inside, she bent down and bit him, nipping with less than gentle teeth, and he growled and didn't bother with her blouse. He unbuckled her belt and shoved down her jeans, unshackling himself, then grabbed her. She leaped and he caught her buttocks in his hands. Her legs wrapped around his waist and Tam, without missing a beat, turned and planted her back against the wall and rammed himself into the sheath of her hot and waiting flesh.

Desi cried out as he drove himself home, all thick heat and power, her arms around his neck, her legs tight around his waist. It was brutal and primitive and when she exploded in orgasm, it was also wildly satisfying. He roared, his body going rigid, and bit down into her shoulder, as if he were an animal, holding her still.

They panted together but didn't speak for long moments. Desi's head fell on his shoulder, and his nose was in her neck, and he held her as if she weighed no more than a little doll.

"We didn't use a condom," Desi said.

He raised his head and met her eyes. "That's because—" he said, and bent to suck her lower lip into his mouth, "—I gave you a baby tonight."

Desi swallowed. "Why would I want a baby with you?"

He grinned and sucked her lip again, running his tongue over the place. "You do." He pulled back and carried her toward the pallet on the floor. "And just to be sure, I think we're gonna do it again."

Desi started to fight him. "What makes you think I want to?"

He laughed, falling down on top of her, catching his weight on his elbows. "Because this is the best sex we've ever had, right here. You fit me," he said, and moved his hips, his member thickening within her in the most erotic feeling Desi had ever known. She couldn't seem to move away, and when he tugged at the hem of her sweater, she let him peel it upward, skimming it over her head, without ever losing touch with their joining. She was there in her bra and nothing else. He still had on boots, and his jeans were around his ankles and his shirt hung open around his bare chest. "And you know it, too," he said gruffly.

Beneath her fingers, his skin felt as sleek and pliant as a horse's flank. She traced a muscle that run from his shoulder to his neck, traced the line up his ear, around his cheekbone, over his eyelid, down to his lower lip. He sucked her finger into his mouth and

Desi felt a rush of anticipation down her spine. "I just don't think I can stand to fall in love, Tam. The only other time just about killed me."

"It wasn't falling in, was it?" he asked reasonably, "It was falling out."

"Yes. That's always the bad part." She sucked in her breath as he brushed his lips over her collarbone and then tried to unfasten the front hook of her bra with one hand. When he wasn't successful, he used both hands. Her breasts tumbled out into the cool air, and he gathered her up.

"Better," he said in a soft voice. His organ twitched, but he stayed still, her thighs on the outside of his, her body clasping his, little echoes of greeting back and forth between them.

He bent to take her nipple into his mouth. "You like this, don't you?"

"What, sex?"

"This part, in particular," he said, and sucked on her nipple, then released it, running his tongue around the tip until there was a low, urgent pulsing between her legs. Around his sex, which simply rested there inside of her, almost too big, stretching her, not moving.

"Yes," she whispered.

"What else?" he said, and raised his head. "What else do you like?"

"About sex?"

"About me."

And in that single second, Desi understood that he was far more vulnerable to her than he let on, that he genuinely wanted to win her good opinion. "So far," she said honestly, looking into the green of his eyes, "I haven't found anything I *don't* like about you, Tamati."

"Yeah?"

"Yeah." She nuzzled closer, rubbed her cheek on his jaw.

"That's what I like to hear," he said, and very slowly, very erotically, began to move.

Later Tam held her close as she dozed. He felt stunned and stung with sweetness and he just held her very close. Quietly, looking into the fire she said, "It's not easy for me to let down my guard, Tam."

"I know, love," he said, and kissed her ear. "I'm patient."

"We can't have a commitment until I know what's going on with the charges against me."

"Why?"

"Because I might go to prison." She rolled over and looked up at him. "You deserve more than sitting around waiting for some woman to get out of jail."

"You deserve more than to go." He half smiled. "What if we run away to New Zealand?"

"Now?"

"No, I'd rather stay here if we can. I love my pub and it'd make my heart sore to leave it, but I think prison would kill you."

A flicker of something sharp crossed her face. "I am afraid of that, too," she admitted. "How could I bear never being outside?" An involuntary shudder moved down her spine. "What do you do inside all day?"

"We won't let it happen, Desdemona. I promise."

Her smile was brittle at the edges. "Even you thought I did it, Tam. There was enough doubt that you would have had to convict me if you'd been on a jury."

"No! I—"

She looked at him. "Don't lie."

He took a breath. "It's a terrible case. We have to find out who did it, that's all."

Desi nodded. "My sister found some great stuff about geothermal conditions," she said, and explained to him about the lake.

Tam whistled. "So what are you going to do?"

"I'm meeting with the reporter tomorrow—and I've been public about it. I hope that strikes some fear into evil ears somewhere."

"Ah."

"And," she said, "I think I'm going to contact all the Native newspapers in the country and see if I can rally some political support."

Her grin was so pleased Tam had to chuckle. He bent and pressed his nose to hers. "In my culture," he said, with a wry little grin, "that is called hongi. Exchanging breath."

She brushed her palm over his cheek, then kissed him. "I like it," she said. "Can we do it again?"

"Absolutely." And when they were pressed close, nose to nose, a wild sense of rightness filled his chest. "If you go to jail, I'll wait for you," he said.

"I don't want to talk about that anymore," she said, then drew back. "But do not leave me sleeping. I hate that."

He chuckled. "You've been mad all day, haven't you?"

"Not mad," she said. "I just hate it."

"Understood." He sighed. "Unfortunately, I have to go tonight. That woman who was at the bar, the skinny one?"

"Skinny A or skinny B?" Desi asked dryly.

"Well, you know Elsa, don't you? The model."

"Oh, good grief. Of course." She rolled her eyes. "It's bad enough your old girlfriend was a beautiful, young blonde. That she's also a recognizable model is a little bit hard to compete with."

"You have no reason to try to compete. You're fantastic."

She raised an eyebrow.

He slid a hand beneath Desi's breast and lifted the luscious heft of it in his palm. "Your breasts are beautiful," he said. "Like you."

She shook her head. "Whatever. I mean, thank you."

He laughed.

"Anyway, the woman? Skinny A, I take it?"

"Right. That's my mate's widow. The one I told you is having a hard time?"

"And?"

He took a breath. "She's sleeping on my couch."

"I see."

It was impossible to tell from her face if this news annoyed or bothered her. "So I should go home."

"All right." She shifted, as if to let him get up.

"Are you irked?"

"No."

"Sure?"

She looked at him. "Do you want me to be?"

He inclined his head slightly. "Well, if you were, I'd have to stay here, wouldn't I?"

Desdemona laughed. "Call her then, and tell her I'll be furious if you go spend the night with another woman in your house. Apartment. Whatever."

He pressed her nose with his own again. "Don't start fretting all over again."

She yawned. "Okay."

His own body returned a yawn, and they fell asleep, wrapped up in a pile like a pair of wolves.

Chapter 14

Desi awakened to Tam kissing her forehead. "I promised not to leave you sleeping, sweet," he said. "Are you awake now? I've got to get to town."

"I am awake," she said. She touched his springy hair, his angled cheekbone. "Thank you for a wonderful evening."

"Second of many," he said, and winked.

Desi wasn't so sure, but she wouldn't argue about it this morning. She was up for a very long jail term. No one should have to commit to that. "Let's take it one day at a time."

"We're going to clear your name, Desdemona. That's a promise."

When he left, she got herself together, made a list

of the things that needed to be done and headed down the mountain. Her first stop was the Red Buffalo Café, which was—as she had anticipated—stuffed to the gills with locals. Skiers tended to eat at their hotels or at the Re-New, so they could get on the slopes as soon as possible. By seven-thirty, the time this morning, they'd already boarded the lifts, leaving behind the core of Natives and long-term locals, and—as she had hoped—the news crews.

She'd been avoiding the local hot spots since Claude's murder and her subsequent arrest, finding the suspicious eyes and gossipy whispers too painful. All of her life, she'd looked for home, and she thought she'd found it in Mariposa. To discover that they'd closed ranks against her over a charming ne'er-do-well like her dead ex had been crushing.

This morning she planned to change that. She wasn't ducking anything or anyone. She would follow her old routines, show up as usual at whatever functions she wished to attend, and to hell with what anyone thought.

"Morning," she said to the rancher in shirtsleeves and cowboy hat at the counter.

"Morning, Doc," he said in his ragged smoker's voice. "Heard you had some trouble last night. Your wolves okay?"

Surprised, but willing to run with it, Desi said, "They're fine. Charles Red Bull and his boys were there, so we only lost one building. Not too bad."

He clicked his tongue. "They got the bastard in custody, though, eh?"

"Yeah. I haven't heard any more."

On the rancher's other side, another man leaned in so he could see Desi around the first man. "I heard they linked it up to Biloxi."

"Really?"

The second man snorted. "Yeah, they want to put in some stupid spa or sumthin', anyway. I get tired of the Californians comin' in here. We got to have some land we're not building up, right?"

Desi nodded, bemused. The waitress came by, a fiftysomething brunette with ropy arms and an impressive bustline. "Mornin', Desi," she said. "We've missed you around here."

She ordered the pancakes and eggs, her stomach growling from the long days and nights she'd been expending so much energy, and ate them while she read the newspaper. All through the meal, people stopped to ask her how she was doing, if the wolves were all right, if she'd lost anything in the fire.

Just like that she was back in the good graces of the town.

Or maybe she'd never been out—maybe her own shame and embarrassment had kept her from finding support in the one place she could count on it: her hometown, the place where she'd found her pack.

Josh, holding Glory's hand, came in as she was getting ready to pay. "Hey! It's good to see you," he said, touching her arm. "Can you sit with us for a little while?"

Glory hugged her legs. "Hi, Auntie. I got a cookbook! You want to see it?"

"Sure," she said to both of them, and went back to a table and sat down. She was expecting a child's cookbook, but it was a glossy guide to thirty-minute meals.

"I love Rachael Ray," Glory said, petting the front of the cookbook. "I want to learn to cook everything in this whole book!"

Desi grinned. "You're just not like anybody else, kiddo, you know that?"

Glory took a deep breath, let it go in a long-suffering sigh. "I know."

"I heard this morning," Josh said, stirring sugar into the coffee the waitress brought over, "that the judge is going to push to get your trial moved up."

The bubble of pleasure around Desi's morning popped, just like that. She bowed her head. "Because he's mad at me," she said. She would have cursed, but mindful of Glory said only, "That...rat."

"We need to look seriously at hiring somebody from the outside."

"Do you have someone in mind?"

"Yes." He pulled a card out of his shirt pocket and passed it over the table. "James Marquez. A buddy of mine from the service."

"I'm game. Let's call him." Her phone rang, and Desi answered it curtly. "Dr. Rousseau."

"Petersons have a colicky horse," Sasha said. "They want you to get right there."

A sick horse was a manageable problem. With relief Desi said, "Tell them I'll be right there." She hung up the phone. "Colicky horse," she said, sliding out of the booth and clipping the phone to her waist again. She kissed Glory's head. "You'll have to cook something for me very soon."

"Okay. You can come over and pick it, and then we'll cook it together!"

"Sounds perfect." To Josh she said, "Call your friend. Get him here. I think I need him."

As she turned to go, one of the ranchers at the counter said in a loud voice, "Hey, Doc, don't let the bastards get you down, you hear?"

She turned, and where she'd seen enemies and trouble, she saw a roomful of faces looking toward her in friendship and support. She raised a hand and waited until she was outside to blink away the tears of gratitude that had gathered.

After she saw the horse, Desi realized she was on the same road that led to the judge's ranch, and in a sudden moment of decision, she headed out to his place.

The day was sunny and clear, and in the exposed areas in front of the house, snow dripped noisily to little rivulets of streams that would freeze and melt, freeze and melt a dozen times more before they melted this summer. At the sound of her truck door slamming, the judge came out of the house.

"I don't have anything to say to you, Desdemona," he said. "Go on back home."

"Well, that's funny," Desi said. "Because I have a few things to say to you." She strode to the step. "All this time I thought you really cared about me, and it was just about the land."

"I gave you a chance to have a good life."

"You mean by marrying you?"

"It could've been a good partnership. We had a lot to offer each other."

Something snapped. "No. I have a lot. You don't have anything to offer me." She glared up at him. "I'm young. I'm healthy. I have all that land that's worth all that money, and now I know there's an aquifer, too. What do you have to offer me?"

His eyes were cold and hard. "I could have offered you protection, you stupid heifer. I *did* offer you protection."

"You just wanted to get laid, Judge," she said, and stepped back. "You wanted a young wife so you could feel like a young man, and if she had plenty of land and money, all the better." She shook her head.

"What would I want with a woman like you, Desdemona? Even an old man can do better than a—" Words failed him and he looked down her body with disdain.

Or what appeared to be disdain. What Desi saw, for the first time, was his lust. He wanted her. Specifically *her*. Her body. Her mouth. Her breasts and hips and legs.

"Nice try," she said, shaking her head. With a gesture she didn't know she had in her, she tugged the rubber band out of her braid and shook her hair free. "You will never have me. Or my land."

"You'll be sorry, Desdemona," he said.

Desi shook her head and turned on her heel, headed back to her truck. It shocked her when he came after her, grabbing her arm and pushing her into the truck. His body pressed into hers. "You still have a chance," he said. "Marry me now and I'll make it all go away. Don't, and I guarantee you'll be sorry."

She met his gaze levelly. "No. Way. You betrayed me worse than my ex-husband. At least I knew he was a player. I trusted you."

He lifted an eyebrow. "More fool you."

Desi didn't move. "Let me go."

For one long moment she didn't know if he would. There was something hot and mean in his eyes, and for long seconds, the possibility of assault was in the air.

Abruptly he let her go. "Get off my land," he growled.

"Gladly," Desi said, and jumped in her truck. By the clock on the dashboard, she saw that she had just enough time to get back to town and meet the reporter at the Black Crown.

Tam served Mick Reed a bottle of Steinlager and asked if he needed anything else. The man shook his head. "I'm just waiting for the vet. She's supposed to meet me here at noon."

"Is that right."

"You think she killed him?" Reed asked, lifting the beer. "Her husband? Sounds like he was a bastard."

"That he was. But she didn't kill him. I don't know who did, but somebody needs to find out."

Desi blew in, a little breathless, her cheeks flushed. She took the stool next to the reporter and cocked her finger toward Tam. He grinned, feeling about fifteen and delighted to be singled out. She stood on the racks of the bar and leaned over the bar and kissed him. "That's so everybody knows I'm your girl, all right?"

He chuckled. "All right. I'm glad to let them know it. You want something? Coffee? Sandwich?"

"No." She grinned at him, then at the reporter. "Let's get started. I have a feeling there might be trouble, and I want this all out in the open."

Reed flipped his notebook to a clean page. "Go."

Desi started talking. Tam heard parts of the story he knew—about her start with Claude and the land they bought and his eventual betrayals. But there were parts he'd not heard—the value of the land, for one thing, the betrayal of the judge who'd offered to marry her, but had done it to get the land. It made him furious.

But that was nothing compared to his fury when two deputies entered the bar and said, "Desdemona Rousseau? You're under arrest for the murder of Claude Tsosie."

She met Tam's eyes with an expression of panic. "I told you there would be trouble. Get my sister over there as fast as possible. Before the bail hearing." The deputy droned on with her Miranda rights, slapping handcuffs on her wrists, leading her out of the bar and into the street where a crowd gathered to watch Desi duck into a patrol car.

They drove away as Tam was picking up the phone. Mick Reed said, "Now this is what I call a story."

"Hang on," Tam said. "There's gonna be more."

* * *

When Nordquist slapped the cold handcuffs around her wrists, Desi felt sick to her stomach. Everything in her protested instantly, deeply. She couldn't stand to go back to that jail!

And yet, there wasn't anything else to do, was there? Feeling panicky, as if she'd awakened in her worst nightmare, she tried to breathe in through her nose, out through her mouth. A roar blocked all the sound in her ears, but she did vaguely notice there were protesters in front of the pub as she came out.

She was booked, once again. Fingerprinted. Again. Put in a holding cell while she waited for the bail hearing. Which probably wouldn't be quite as good this time, since she'd been officially charged.

The room was cold and grim, lit with greenish light. There was a scent of old vomit and cigarettes in the walls, and she wondered again how long it would take for the smell of smoke to dissipate— smoking hadn't been allowed indoors in Mariposa for years. In one corner, a young woman with a black eye lay back on a bench, ignoring Desi.

Which suited Desi just fine. She bent over her hands and spread them open, peering at the lines on her palms for clues to the future. Once, a gypsy at a carnival had told her she had the mark of destiny on her Mount of Venus, that she would do "great things." Desi ran her right index finger over the place where a multipointed star marked the fleshy pad beneath her left index finger. She hadn't had the heart to tell the gypsy that the mark was a scar. She'd fallen off her trike when she was five and landed just right on a little rock. It left a mark for all time.

Destiny.

Despair, black and thick as tar, closed in on her. How could she breathe in a prison cell for the rest of her life? How could she possibly face such a life, knowing everything she had lost out there?

One of which was Tam.

She had prayed so much and so often to so many deities now that she had no faith or words left. There was only one word.

Please.

Tam frantically chased down Juliet and found her at work. When he told her what was happening, she first went white, then kicked back her chair. Smoothing her hair, she said, "How many reporters are in town?"

He grinned. "Hey, Hollywood. I like the way you think."

"Find every last one of them," she said. "They've been looking for a story. Let's give them one."

So he went to the hotel and stopped in the pubs and sent Amy up the ski slopes to see if there were any others up there. They assembled at the Black Crown, and Juliet was absolutely comfortable as she took her place at the front of the group. "Thanks, all of you, for coming," she said. "I know you've all been hoping for a story, and I think you finally got it—but it's a lot more sensational than a little love triangle, even if it does involve one of the prettiest skiers to ever ski a slope."

An appreciative laugh met her words.

"The real story here is not about a woman who killed her husband, but a woman who is sitting on some of the most valuable land to be discovered since the gold rush. A woman who is being harassed and framed and vandalized." Juliet passed out a piece of paper with facts about the land values in Mariposa County, and about the plot of land Desi was sitting on in particular. The burly reporter from this morning whistled softly.

The door burst open and three men came in. Tam recognized Bill Biloxi, a square-faced man with the red flush of someone about to have a heart attack any second, and Judge Alexander Yancy, a sixty-something man with a grizzling of white hair. The third man was trim and well-to-do, but Tam was fairly sure he'd never seen him before.

They listened as the reporters asked questions. A cop from the sheriff's office raised his hand and protested. "We're not trying to make an example out of her," he said. "There's a lot of evidence against her."

A rancher spoke up. "Then give her a damned trial and let a jury of her peers decide. That girl didn't kill Claude Tsosie, and everybody in this room damned well knows it."

A dark-haired woman—Tam thought it might be Alice Turner—said, "I don't know that. She was evil to her husband."

"Give her a trial or leave her alone!" someone else cried.

Noise rose and swelled, shouts and protests and

even feet stomping. Juliet let it rise and rise, then held up a hand. "The reporters have more questions," she said.

"Is it true, Judge Yancy, that you hired a henchman to torch the wolf center?"

"Don't be ridiculous!" the judge blustered, but the noise level rose even higher.

Tam crossed his arms. "What about asking her to marry you, Judge?" he called out. "And I hear she turned you down. How about that?"

The judge shook his head, pretending dignity, but everyone in the room knew the story was won. And finally, Desi would be out of jail within hours. She might not even, if they were lucky, have to stand trial.

Chapter 15

The night was bright and cold, with a moon shining hard into the clearing by the hot springs. The women gathered by the fire that had been built earlier this afternoon and kept very hot so the stones could be heated in the coals.

Desi would stand trial for the murder of Claude Tsosie, which was why they had gathered here tonight. Desi kept her hands crossed over her chest, ready to make peace with all that had happened and empty herself so she could face whatever might be next. There had not been any new evidence, so Juliet was optimistic any jury of her peers would throw the case out, but one never knew.

Despite a great deal of pressure, there had also

been no evidence to connect the judge or Biloxi to the vandalism and arson and attacks at the wolf center. With resignation, Desi had hired more guards and intended to stay with it as long as necessary.

The others gave her space, seeming to understand that she could not bear one more platitude, one more well-meant condolence.

There were seven women tonight, both Anglo and Indian. Helene, who was their teacher, stood before the lodge with a fan of eagle feathers in her hands. Next to her was a short, round woman with long silver braids called Desmary, and her daughter, Margaret, and her sister in law, Paula, who was cousin to Alex and Josh and Glory, so technically, an almost relative to Juliet, who stood next to Desi, shivering. The final member of the group, Kelly, was tall and lean and solemn. It was she who built and tended the fire and the stones for the sweat lodge.

Helene opened the ceremony and they entered the lodge one at a time, quietly taking their places in the dark. Then Kelly brought in stones and piled them in a little hollow in the middle of the sweat lodge, and their heat filled the small, low room quickly. Kelly scooted back in and pulled the flap behind her. Helene sprinkled sweetgrass over the glowing hot stones, and tiny sparks burst in the unbroken darkness.

Desi breathed in the familiar, ancient scent and something within her unfurled. Here in the darkness, she could rest with spirits of the directions, the spirits of her ancestors, and the animals' spirits and mother earth. Nothing had to be decided. Nothing had to be tended. Here she could release everything.

Then came the steam and the songs and the stories, the prayers and petitions and offerings. Desi let the familiar rituals soothe her, knowing she would eventually come to whatever she was meant to do, too.

Next to her, the ritual proved cleansing for Juliet, who'd been trying to let go of terrible memories about a rape. Desi felt her sister weeping with relief and release, a healing and powerful sound. She did not touch her, did not interfere. The spirits did what they did. On Juliet's other side was Zara, the widow Tam had taken under his wing. She was wide-eyed and quiet, but Desi knew it was a good step.

When it was Desi's turn, she knew suddenly that it was her marriage she was to surrender, in all its illusion and beauty, foolishness and honor, peace and anger. For a long, long moment she sat in the dark and smelled sweetgrass and steam and sweat, and all of it filled her. Conflicting images of joy and despair. Making love and making a home and laughing. Fighting furiously, hurting each other, weeping.

The memories seemed to almost take the shape of a body, and Desi closed her eyes and embraced it, the whole marriage, the whole of her time with Claude. Then, consciously, she lowered her arms and mentally said, "Thank you. You may go."

The body stood and leaped into the air and flew away.

Desi bent her head and wept.

And when she was done, she felt ten thousand times lighter. Wiser. Better. Now she could go forward.

Funny how it was very clear what direction she should go.

Tam had received an invitation to go to dinner at Desi's cabin via her sister, who brought the card in an envelope. "Please come to dinner on Friday, March 13," it read. "A jacket and tie would not be out of place."

With some amusement, Tam scoured his closet for a suit, and found a brown one with dusty shoulders in the very, very back. He couldn't even remember when he'd worn it last. Maybe for Roger's funeral. He hated to wear something with such unpleasant memories to what promised to be a festive occasion, but there wasn't anything else. He jazzed it up with a purple tie, and bought some daffodils at the grocery store, a nice bunch of spring flowers to carry up the mountain.

The dogs went crazy inside the cabin, and as Tam stepped out of the truck, he smelled the heady aroma of roasting meat. He saw Desi's head in the window and the warm lamplight spilling out. For one moment he paused, his chest aching at the homey sight. He was so ready to settle down, and not just for the sake of it, but because he'd searched the world over, like Magellan, for the secret of life and had found it in Desdemona Rousseau. He'd probably known the instant he first saw her, weeping over a wolf she couldn't save.

He knocked on the door and she opened it with a

grin. "Come in, Tamati," she said. "Oh, the flowers are lovely!"

But for a minute he couldn't move. She was dressed in a—well, a *dress*. A blue cotton dress with a full skirt and a belt at the waist, very sixties suburban unless he missed his guess. On her feet were high heels and her legs were spectacular. "Wow. Great legs, babe."

"Thanks. Won't you come in?"

He followed her in, noting more little oddities. The table was set with matching plates and silver, and her hair was swept up into some doodad on the back of her head. Some kind of bun or something. And— "Are those pearls around your neck?" he asked.

Desi spun around like a game-show girl. "Yes. What do you think?"

He peered at her. "I think I might be in the wrong house."

She grinned, and he saw in the impish expression the Desi he knew. "Why, Tamati," she said with mocking severity. "I'm only connecting with my own culture. Please, sit down. I've made roast beef."

He took a chair and let her serve him, trying to keep his lips from forming a smile. She served perfectly sliced beef, a side of mashed potatoes with brown gravy, peas that had come from a can, brown-and-serve rolls and butter. With Kool-Aid.

Her eyes dancing, she sat down with him and put her napkin in her lap. "In my culture," she said, "this is what women do to win the heart of a man.

I read it in all the magazines." She sampled the meat and urged him to do the same. "Isn't it delicious, dear?"

He tasted it and had to agree. But he couldn't relax until he figured out what—

"I suppose," she said, "it does depend on what magazine you read."

"Yeah?"

She nodded, serious. "Some say the way to a man's heart is through his stomach." She flipped up her fluffy skirt and wiggled an eyebrow. "Some say it's through something else—and just in case, I'm not wearing any underwear."

"Now you're talking my language," he said. He put down his fork. "What about the heart method, Desdemona? Are there magazines that talk about that?"

"Not really," she said. "In my culture, it isn't thought that men have hearts."

"I see." He met her eyes. "What if I want to marry you, Desi?"

She bit her lip. "I told you, I can't marry you until we know whether I'm going to jail or not. But in the meantime, I'm willing to be your adoring girlfriend."

His heart pinched. "Girlfriend?"

"Yes." Her eyes sparkled. "And maybe…the mother of your child?"

He went still. "What?"

Her grin was as wide as the mountain sky. "Yep. Confirmed, my dear. You said you were going to get me pregnant, and you did."

Tam gaped.

Desi took a bite of her roast beef. "Lucky for me I found a man with a heart."

With a roar of happiness, Tam jumped up and took her in his arms and kissed her. Her lips. Her face. Her neck. "This makes me happy, Desi. Very happy."

"Me, too, Tam. Whatever happens we'll have done this one thing."

He buried his face in her neck. She would not go to jail. He would never allow it. Never. "I love you," he whispered. "I had to search the wide, wide world for you, and I'm not giving you up, you hear me?"

"I'm glad you searched, Tam. And I love you," she said, gripping him in return with her strong arms. "How lucky for me to have found a man with a heart."

He hugged her close, his strapping love, who filled up his arms and filled up his heart and filled up his life.

He was home.

* * * * *

Set in darkness beyond the ordinary world.
Passionate tales of life and death.
With characters' lives ruled by laws the everyday
world can't begin to imagine.

n●cturne

It's time to discover the Raintree trilogy....

New York Times bestselling author
LINDA HOWARD
brings you the dramatic first book
RAINTREE: INFERNO

The Ansara Wizards are rising and the Raintree
clan must rejoin the battle against their foes, testing
their powers, relationships and forcing upon them
lives they never could have imagined before....

Turn the page for a sneak preview
of the captivating first book
in the Raintree trilogy,
RAINTREE: INFERNO by LINDA HOWARD
On sale April 25.

Dante Raintree stood with his arms crossed as he watched the woman on the monitor. The image was in black and white to better show details; color distracted the brain. He focused on her hands, watching every move she made, but what struck him most was how uncommonly *still* she was. She didn't fidget or play with her chips, or look around at the other players. She peeked once at her down card, then didn't touch it again, signaling for another hit by tapping a fingernail on the table. Just because she didn't seem to be paying attention to the other players, though, didn't mean she was as unaware as she seemed.

"What's her name?" Dante asked.

"Lorna Clay," replied his chief of security, Al Rayburn.

"At first I thought she was counting, but she doesn't pay enough attention."

"She's paying attention, all right," Dante murmured. "You just don't see her doing it." A card counter had to remember every card played. Supposedly counting cards was impossible with the number of decks used by the casinos, but there were those rare individuals who could calculate the odds even with multiple decks.

"I thought that, too," said Al. "But look at this piece of tape coming up. Someone she knows comes up to her and speaks, she looks around and starts chatting, completely misses the play of the people to her left—and doesn't look around even when the deal comes back to her, just taps that finger. And damn if she didn't win. Again."

Dante watched the tape, rewound it, watched it again. Then he watched it a third time. There had to be something he was missing, because he couldn't pick out a single giveaway.

"If she's cheating," Al said with something like respect, "she's the best I've ever seen."

"What does your gut say?"

Al scratched the side of his jaw, considering. Finally, he said, "If she isn't cheating, she's the luckiest person walking. She wins. Week in, week out, she wins. Never a huge amount, but I ran the numbers and she's into us for about five grand a week. Hell, boss, on her way out of the casino she'll stop by a slot machine, feed a dollar in and walk away with at least fifty. It's never the same machine, either. I've had her watched, I've had her followed, I've even looked for the same faces in the casino every time she's in here, and I can't find a common denominator."

"Is she here now?"

"She came in about a half hour ago. She's playing blackjack, as usual."

"Bring her to my office," Dante said, making a swift decision. "Don't make a scene."

"Got it," said Al, turning on his heel and leaving the security center.

Dante left, too, going up to his office. His face was calm. Normally he would leave it to Al to deal with a cheater, but he was curious. How was she doing it? There were a lot of bad cheaters, a few good ones, and every so often one would come along who was the stuff of which legends were made: the cheater who didn't get caught, even when people were alert and the camera was on him—or, in this case, her.

It was possible to simply be lucky, as most people understood luck. Chance could turn a habitual loser into a big-time winner. Casinos, in fact, thrived on that hope. But luck itself wasn't habitual, and he knew that what passed for luck was often something else: cheating. And there was the other kind of luck, the kind he himself possessed, but it depended not on chance but on who and what he was. He knew it was an innate power and not Dame Fortune's erratic smile. Since power like his was rare, the odds made it likely the woman he'd been watching was merely a very clever cheat.

Her skill could provide her with a very good living, he thought, doing some swift calculations in his head. Five grand a week equaled $260,000 a year, and that was just from his casino. She probably hit them all, careful to keep the numbers relatively low so she stayed under the radar.

He wondered how long she'd been taking him, how long she'd been winning a little here, a little there, before Al noticed.

The curtains were open on the wall-to-wall window in his office, giving the impression, when one first opened the door, of stepping out onto a covered balcony. The glazed window faced west, so he could catch the sunsets. The sun was low now, the sky painted in purple and gold. At his home in the mountains, most of the windows faced east, affording him views of the sunrise. Something in him needed both the greeting and the goodbye of the sun. He'd always been drawn to sunlight, maybe because fire was his element to call, to control.

He checked his internal time: four minutes until sundown. Without checking the sunrise tables every day, he knew exactly when the sun would slide behind the mountains. He didn't own an alarm clock. He didn't need one. He was so acutely attuned to the sun's position that he had only to check within himself to know the time. As for waking at a particular time, he was one of those people who could tell himself to wake at a certain time, and he did. That talent had nothing to do with being Raintree, so he didn't have to hide it; a lot of perfectly ordinary people had the same ability.

He had other talents and abilities, however, that did require careful shielding. The long days of summer instilled in him an almost sexual high, when he could feel contained power buzzing just beneath his skin. He had to be doubly careful not to cause candles to leap into flame just by his presence, or to start wildfires with a glance in the dry-as-tinder brush. He loved Reno; he didn't want to burn it down. He just felt so damn *alive* with all the sunshine pouring down that he wanted to let the energy pour through him instead of holding it inside.

This must be how his brother Gideon felt while pulling lightning, all that hot power searing through his muscles, his veins. They had this in common, the connection with raw power. All the members of the far-flung Raintree clan had some power, some heightened ability, but only members of the royal family could channel and control the earth's natural energies.

Dante wasn't just of the royal family, he was the Dranir, the leader of the entire clan. "Dranir" was synonymous with king, but the position he held wasn't ceremonial, it was one of sheer power. He was the oldest son of the previous Dranir, but he would have been passed over for the position if he hadn't also inherited the power to hold it.

Behind him came Al's distinctive knock on the door. The outer office was empty, Dante's secretary having gone home hours before. "Come in," he called, not turning from his view of the sunset.

The door opened, and Al said, "Mr. Raintree, this is Lorna Clay."

Dante turned and looked at the woman, all his senses on alert. The first thing he noticed was the vibrant color of her hair, a rich, dark red that encompassed a multitude of shades from copper to burgundy. The warm amber light danced along the iridescent strands, and he felt a hard tug of sheer lust in his gut. Looking at her hair was almost like looking at fire, and he had the same reaction.

The second thing he noticed was that she was spitting mad.

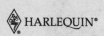

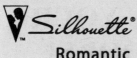

Romantic
SUSPENSE

**Sparked by Danger,
Fueled by Passion.**

*This month and every month look for
four new heart-racing romances
set against a backdrop of suspense!*

Available in May 2007

Safety in Numbers
(*Wild West Bodyguards miniseries*)
by **Carla Cassidy**

Jackson's Woman
by **Maggie Price**

Shadow Warrior
(*Night Guardians miniseries*)
by **Linda Conrad**

One Cool Lawman
by **Diane Pershing**

Available wherever you buy books!

Visit Silhouette Books at www.eHarlequin.com

REQUEST YOUR FREE BOOKS!

2 FREE NOVELS PLUS 2 FREE GIFTS!

Silhouette® Romantic

SUSPENSE

Sparked by Danger, Fueled by Passion!

YES! Please send me 2 FREE Silhouette® Romantic Suspense novels and my 2 FREE gifts. After receiving them, if I don't wish to receive any more books, I can return the shipping statement marked "cancel." If I don't cancel, I will receive 4 brand-new novels every month and be billed just $4.24 per book in the U.S., or $4.99 per book in Canada, plus 25¢ shipping and handling per book plus applicable taxes, if any*. That's a savings of at least 15% off the cover price! I understand that accepting the 2 free books and gifts places me under no obligation to buy anything. I can always return a shipment and cancel at any time. Even if I never buy another book from Silhouette, the two free books and gifts are mine to keep forever.

240 SDN EEX6 340 SDN EEYJ

Name	(PLEASE PRINT)

Address	Apt. #

City	State/Prov.	Zip/Postal Code

Signature (if under 18, a parent or guardian must sign)

Mail to the **Silhouette Reader Service™:**
IN U.S.A.: P.O. Box 1867, Buffalo, NY 14240-1867
IN CANADA: P.O. Box 609, Fort Erie, Ontario L2A 5X3

Not valid to current Silhouette Intimate Moments subscribers.

Want to try two free books from another line?
Call 1-800-873-8635 or visit www.morefreebooks.com.

* Terms and prices subject to change without notice. NY residents add applicable sales tax. Canadian residents will be charged applicable provincial taxes and GST. This offer is limited to one order per household. All orders subject to approval. Credit or debit balances in a customer's account(s) may be offset by any other outstanding balance owed by or to the customer. Please allow 4 to 6 weeks for delivery.

Your Privacy: Silhouette is committed to protecting your privacy. Our Privacy Policy is available online at www.eHarlequin.com or upon request from the Reader Service. From time to time we make our lists of customers available to reputable firms who may have a product or service of interest to you. If you would prefer we not share your name and address, please check here. ☐

SRS07

COMING NEXT MONTH

#1463 SAFETY IN NUMBERS—Carla Cassidy
Wild West Bodyguards
Chase McCall arrives in Cotter Creek to investigate the powerful entity of bodyguards known as the West family and immediately strikes an attraction for the lone female of the bunch. Can Chase keep his cool while exploring these possible murder suspects?

#1464 JACKSON'S WOMAN—Maggie Price
Dates with Destiny
U.S. special agent Jackson Castle watched Claire Munroe walk away from him once. Now his ex-partner vows vengeance on him by going after the only woman he's ever loved…and Jackson is all that stands between Claire and a cold-blooded killer.

#1465 SHADOW WARRIOR—Linda Conrad
Night Guardians
Tradition demands that Michael Ayze marry his brother's widow—the woman he's forbidden to love. Will Michael resist temptation and still protect Alexis from the evil shapeshifters who will use her for ill?

#1466 ONE COOL LAWMAN—Diane Pershing
Can an L.A. detective fight his attraction to the mother of a kidnapped girl long enough to uncover the perpetrator? In doing so, he's risking his life—but can he also handle risking his heart?